VEG

VEG

Zachery Lawrence Nims

Download the free App: VEG Gaming Evolved from I-tunes or Google Play on your smart phone today! Follow the INFO button instructions and enjoy.

First Printing: 2016

ISBN 978-0-9972020-0-7

Zachery Nims
2224 E 20th Street
Tulsa, OK 74104

www.facebook.com/virtualearthgrid/

Ordering Information:

Special discounts are available on quantity purchases by corporations, associations, educators, and others. For details, contact the publisher at the above listed address.

U.S. trade bookstores and wholesalers: Please contact VEG.GamingEvolved@gmail.com

Dedication

To my wife Lauren: Whose heavy snoring forced me to stay up writing. Without your encouragement, I would have never finished this novel. You are my heart, my lover, my Lauren.

To my parents: Thank you for nurturing the strange and weird sides of your sons.

To my brother Todd: I am lucky to have a brother that is also my best friend. Thank you for your protection, support, and friendship. I look forward to our adventures together.

To the new Augmented Reality Pokemon Game released in 2016 that is just like my novel: Thank you Pikachu, for forcing me to publish this novel ahead of schedule. If it isn't well received, I blame your adorable little yellow face.

Contents

Acknowledgements

I would like to thank all of my Kickstarter backers without whose help this book would never have been completed.

A special thanks to the following people:

Todd Nims
Don & Cherry Nims
Bryant Hebert
Grant Manthey
Rick & Gail Hebard
David Elliott
William Izmirlian

These few are the true philanthropists in life. The ones that encourage dreams and inspire hope in humanity. It is not often that you run into such individuals. We shy away from such strength. I'm fortunate to call some of these people my friends and even more fortunate to call some family. Thank you for all your help and I hope that one day, I will be able to support you as you have supported me.

Chapter 1: The Golden Years
Source: Blog Entry
Name: Mastablasta

William Higinbotham, with an analog computer, created the very first video game called 'Pong' in 1985. With 700 pounds of equipment and an oscilloscope screen, three components lit up with a neon green glow on a grid resembling a two-dimensional tennis match. It was fitting that the first video game was displayed on a grid, for a grid was what now engulfed the earth.

In the beginning games advanced at a relatively slow rate. There weren't gamers, just merely people finding yet another way to occupy their time. As games advanced, the vox populi was that they would become an escape from the world and ultimately lead to our individual isolation. We became infatuated with the idea of virtual reality pods as an attainable future. These stationary cells would allow users to have all of the sensations of the real world within the confines of their home. An idea built upon the backs of a rising slothful race. It was an enticing concept to some but adversarial to humanity. Science fiction novels and films glorified this idea. Massively multiplayer online games or MMO's began to isolate our race even further, gripping the youth with the newest form of gaming heroin. It flooded the veins of every nation and human interaction began its ultimate decline.

Our society started to cater to our isolation by providing us with online shopping and automated kiosks so that one could spend an entire day without truly having to speak to or acknowledge anyone. We indulged in guilty secretive pleasures and succumbed to our primal interests. It made our race easy to control and even easier to manipulate. Our economy fell out from under us giving way to a generation that would rather rot away in their virtual haven than work for a living.

We were breeding a race that fed off instant gratification. Patience was a rare virtue as time progressed. People decided that if it took longer than a minute to satisfy their need, than the fault lay with the other individual. "I hate stupid people," was a phrase that took off due to the impatience of the youth. Unemployment levels sky rocketed and it became common practice for parents to support their children well into their thirties. Our arrogance allowed us to neglect the "sink or swim" concept and to coddle the youth until we crippled them. Everyone had a source to blame for their own shortcomings. It was easier to point the finger than to accept that we weren't preparing our children for the battle of life. Every animal knows the true meaning of survival of the fittest but it is human nature to play god and allow everyone a crippling chance. Obesity ran rampant, as did a bombardment of psychological "diseases". Therapists, psychiatrists, and psychologists were a dime a dozen. Our future looked bleak.

Then VEG hit the market, created by a visionary named Charles Sanders who saw a light at the end of the darkness. Charles invented the first system that stimulated our economy. At this point, China had become the economic leader. The Chinese Yuan was the leading currency in the world market. The US, with a declining economy, began to fear a hostile takeover. We had no way to compete with China because we had exhausted all our natural resources. Our oil embargo had diminished its hold due to our environmental policies. We wouldn't allow refineries on our own soil so we outsourced jobs overseas and paid dearly for it. This combined with the rise in sustainable energies caused a final bust for oil that wasn't cost effective for us to wean off of. The rest of the world profited while our economy imploded upon itself. The only advantage America held onto was its innovation. We excelled in futurism, current fashion, and art. Leading the world in designing business models helped us, but they were sold for next to nothing.

VEG changed everything. No one knew how to react to it at first. Its premiering advertisement was bizarre. It showed an overweight boy sitting next to a screen that encompassed his entire wall. It was motion based but could also be played with a console controller.

The room depicted an average middle class household. The design was modern, and the decor made the little room feel spacious. The boy's mother entered with a package, "William that game that you ordered just arrived!" If it weren't for William's poor physique he would have been ripping the box open in a matter of seconds. One could only see the excitement on his face but his body suggested otherwise. He rolled around like a bowling ball until his knees were under him. Shaking furiously, he used all four limbs to lift his hefty mass to a standing position. Out of breath, he staggered over to the box where the giant red letters VEG were branded on top.

Inside, the contents were simple: a pair of clear glasses, four pads for the knees and elbows, and a device that looked like a lightsaber. The glasses would later be known as "Jackers" and the lightsaber as "the rod," which would allow for countless hours of "that's what she said" jokes.

The boy put on his glasses and pads. He then grabbed his rod and opened the front door. As the door opened, a high concentration of bright contrasted light poured through, as if a portal to another world had appeared. The boy walked out, barely fitting through the door's frame. It closed and reopened in an instant, but where once stood a boy, was now a huge, heavily armed adult, carrying spoils from across the universe. The man took off his Jackers and all of his armor disappeared leaving a lean, toned male in his mid-twenties, baring the faint resemblance of the boy who stepped outside.

Although confusing, the commercial left an air of mystery. Most of the gaming forums had no idea what to make of it but they began researching Charles Sanders and littered the Internet with information on the man. He was a computer programming wiz with radical ideas, which had locked himself away for over twenty years. He was said to have been programming with a team of interns but every intern was sworn to secrecy. That was until the E3 exposition in 2018.

E3 is a gaming forum that draws gamers from all over the world. This particular forum was a little different than it had historically been. The turnout was enormous, but the main difference was that every attendee had to go through a series of tests using a pair of glasses that looked just like the ones in the VEG commercial. Once the glasses were placed on the individuals face they were asked a series of questions as the glasses calculated their body's dimensions. They then stepped on a scale so their weight could be calculated. Next they were asked to tilt their head to its limit in every direction. To finish, each individual chose his or her character type, healer, mage, warrior, rogue, and so on. Then they were given glasses, rod, pads and granted entrance.

The stadium was set up in a peculiar manner. Charles Sanders stood in the center of a hexagon floor panel. Metal poles were erected on the corners connected by lasers. It appeared to be a battle arena. Attendees were instructed not to cross the laser barrier but that didn't stop the crowd from rushing to stand at its perimeter. They fought like children for a spot to view Charles, the programmer that hadn't been seen in public for twenty years.

The man had aged quite a bit from the pictures that had been flooding the Internet. Charles stood now with a pasty white complexion before an eagerly awaiting crowd of thousands. His whitish gray facial hair ran rampant resembling the wolf man just before total transformation. He was an eccentric old hermit that looked like he hadn't bathed in a week. He spoke suddenly, his voice sounding like a god, roaring down from all angles of the structure, "Greetings gamers of outdated and obsolete technologies, I present you the final gaming frontier. A gift that will change not only your gaming experience but also the world in which you live, and I assure you that it will exceed all expectations."

With a flick of his fingers, he manifested a glowing earth in the palm of his right hand. It was an augmented three-dimensional hologram that could only be seen with the VEG glasses on. Astonishment hung over the crowd as he increased its size. Just like the oscilloscope screen for pong, the earth had a grid covering its entirety. "The Virtual Earth Grid stands before you, or as I like to call it, VEG. I, along with many others, have been designing and programming our actual earth on a grid. Any player that registers, as you all have today, now has access to our earth as a completely immersive gaming environment."

Charles was wide eyed with excitement but was met with puzzled expressions. "Let me show you a little bit more of what I mean." He then pulled out his rod and clicked the large red button near his trigger finger. In an instant, beautiful armor covered his entire body. The rod turned into a giant flaming sword that he waved in a circular motion creating a spinning ring of fire. When you took your glasses off, it all disappeared, but with them on you could see the gleaming reds from his armor, the fire twirling around the steel of his sword, so realistic that you could barely distinguish what was reality and what was virtual.

"BEGIN," Charles roared. Instantaneously, six giant ogre beasts appeared out of thin air and surrounded him. Charles ran at the first one sliding on his knees underneath the ogre's melee attack, a club blanketed with metal spikes. Charles sliced at its right Achilles tendon sending him crashing to the ground. The ogre grabbed his ankle and screamed. In a desperate folly, he hurled his monstrous club toward Charles's head. Charles pushed another button on his rod that casted a colossal wall of ice in front of him. The ice shield cracked upon impact, misdirecting the club just inches overhead.

Placing the rod to his lips, Charles began chanting foreign sounding words over and over again as the other five ogres approached. A fire began to grow five yards out from him that stopped the ogres dead in their tracks. His chanting became louder and louder until the fire erupted. From its core, came an enormous red dragon, breathing down fiery death. It landed on the sixth crippled ogres head, crushing its skull with the weight of his massive body. Thick, green goo sprayed out in every direction staining Charles's armor. Charles slammed his sword into the ground and the earth split, cracking underneath its force. He put his arms out toward the heavens, turning slow in celebration of his victory. Then he pushed another button on his rod and everything disappeared.

"For the first time in the history of gaming you will be using your entire body to interact with the world around you. Our Earth is now your playground!" He snapped his fingers again and an image of a park appeared with kids playing VEG battling a troll looking creature. "Imagine battling a boss on the peak of Mount Kilimanjaro. Imagine scuba diving in the Bahamas on a shipwreck, attacking a sea serpent that guards an elite item called The Gauntlets of Atlantis. Imagine sky diving over Middle America to farm flying creatures for an epic quest." An electric buzz began to fill the air. The crowd was in awe as images flashed before them of what was possible. "You will be awarded not only with levels and treasures but also by how agile and honed your skills become. I promise you that this game is the first step to us all becoming the healthiest country on the face of the planet. Gamers will be idolized inside and outside of the gaming community. You will possess talents that no one will understand, you will climb the tallest mountains, you will explore the deepest caves, and best of all you will face your deepest fears." With that everyone erupted in applause. It was the greatest game anyone had ever seen.

A cable came down from the ceiling. Charles grabbed it and began to float away, exiting the arena but when he reached the ceiling he spoke one last time. "I have given you all base armor and beginners weapons. Please prepare yourself for war. If you die you will not get to keep your VEG gear. If you survive then I bid you a good journey and happy hunting." Smiling, he vanished through a door in the roof of the structure.

The crowd was left in silence waiting with anticipation. It built to the point that it awakened fear in the heart. Then, without warning, the barrier of lasers disappeared from the central arena and the ground began to tremble. The lights went out and darkness swam in. Screams lurked from gloomy corners, sending the flock of humans into panic. Ones in the center called for visual descriptions of the horrors that crept in the pitch-black room. Their questions answered with limp lifeless bodies being lobbed from the darkness into the center of the arena. The bodies were virtual projections of the user being thrown. The game had an incredible amount of physics built into it. The avatar of the player flew away while the physical user stood stunned, frozen in place. It took a couple of seconds for the virtual body to warp back to the original location and then the user was given full mobility again. Having your body thrown was essentially a prolonged stun.

Aliens, dark and disfigured Picasso rejects, emerged from the shadows. They were three times the size of men and mucus colored, their skin partially transparent. When they quivered you could almost see through them. Their heads were scaled like a dragon's with elongated noses and great big round eyes. The core of their body was unique in that each of them had enlarged potbellies. The potbellies being so big that it affected the way they walked. They hobbled toward the panicking crowd, coddling their bellies like a prized possession. Then one of the Aliens screamed, throwing his head back. His stomach exploded, sending four miniature flying aliens airborne. They were a fifth the size of their host with dragonfly wings and two sharp raptor-like claws on each hand. They didn't bide their time before attacking. They leapt onto the chest of a warrior standing idly by and ripped open his belly, fighting over his entrails.

After the rabid creatures finished their intestinal meal, one of them hopped inside his stomach, sealing it up with some sort of heat mending technique. During the fighting the users found that the VEG elbow pads and kneepads not only oriented where the user was for the augmented overlay of their armor but it also could paralyze their body parts with electric shock. When a monster hacked off your leg it would become paralyzed and useless. The man lay frozen on the ground while an augmented virtual circus was taking place on his body. Unable to move, he looked on in horror as his belly began to grow from the larva developing within. It was so realistic looking that a couple of the younger users began crying.

People started pushing buttons on their rods and all of the sudden there were warriors, mages, and rogues. Wands, bows, and swords were beginning to appear along with daggers and battle·axes. The aliens eyed the crowd, a little more wary than before, seeing the newly acquired armor and weapons. They barked orders at each other from across the room, like dogs advising on strategy for the hunt.

Then one man in the crowd, a little on the heavy side, let out a cry, "ATTACK," as he ran at the one closest to him. The alien parried but was too surprised from the strike to have sure footing. It was like a mouse attacking an elephant and the alien was caught in the shock of the moment. He took a clumsy step back, losing balance as he protected his wobbling potbelly. The man swung his axe hard into the alien's left leg chopping it clear off. This sent it falling to the ground, its right arm extended outwards to brace for impact. But the warrior was there to strike it. He landed a blow that collapsed the joint causing the alien to slam into the ground.

The heavy set man was now wheezing a bit but was too entranced by the idea of finishing the alien off to care. He raised his axe and just before he could bring it down upon its throat a bombardment of arrows pierced the alien's skull. The man turned, ripe with anger, to yell at the archers for stealing his glory. However before he could, four aliens leapt from the deceased's belly, ripping the axe wielding warrior's chest open while gnawing at his throat. One jumped inside the heavy-set man and began sewing. His belly was already enormous so you couldn't see the effect of the hive inside of him until minutes later. The two dead users now sat with enlarged puss pod like bellies ready to explode. The human body was smaller than the Aliens, so the embryos stretched the skin out so thin that you could see the gestation occurring. Cells were splitting at the rate of rapid-growth bacteria, forming grotesque abominations that slithered around each other, trying to break free of their paper-thin womb. The skin couldn't contain their movement and they burst out prematurely, screaming as they rode a wave of stomach fluids onto the ground. Although not airborne yet, as their wings hadn't been given enough time to fully develop, they were still quick as rabbits leaping around on all fours. This was all a virtual show at this point. The physical person was removed from the arena once his character was announced dead. He sat as a spectator, watching with frustration as the aliens hatched from his augmented replica's core. It was so realistic that it looked as if his twin was there in front of him.

A group of four users figured out a way to contain their monster. They had a frost mage, who focused all of her freezing spells on the belly when the Alien died. It contained the embryos long enough for a hunter to wrap the body in a metal mesh trap. Then a fire mage ignited the belly ensuring that everything burned within. They downed two but before the group fought another, an alien approached from their rear. It ripped off one of the hunter's shoulder plates, throwing it into an archer's chest. The alien swung high hitting the hunter across the face sending his body soaring across the room. The impact only caused minor damage, a healer already running to aid him. The other three took control, using ice to trap both of the alien's feet while a couple players attacked it from behind sending its body lunging forward. Its arms tried to protect its stomach but before they could, warriors chopped them off. Without their bracing, the impact was fatal, not only to itself but also to the underdeveloped soft skinned alien babies within its belly. People worried that the goo might be acidic, running at first, but it only blinded their Jackers. Users delighted in the fact that they had to physically wipe the augmented mucus off their glasses with their hands before they could see again. VEG had considered everything in the programming. It was these subtle touches that made the whole environment so beautiful.

The crowd began understanding how to use their characters and within minutes all of the aliens were dead with only twenty user fatalities. The crowd was excited and breathing heavily but also patting each other on the back, thanking and congratulating one another. The victory was short lived.

The room went dark, and a voice boomed from the darkness. "STEP AWAY FROM THE CENTER OF THE ROOM. ZOGON THE DESTROYER ARRIVES." Red lights began to flash and a blinding beam shot down from the ceiling. When it disappeared, an enormous black-scaled half dragon half pit-bull looking boss stood in its place. He laughed loudly, "THIS IS ALL EARTH HAS TO OFFER?" He grabbed the first person he saw, picking him off the ground. He toyed with the user for a second before tossing their body against the far wall as if it weighed nothing. The character's hit points dropped to zero, killing him instantly. Of course he didn't truly throw the character but Zogon picked up and threw the augmented reality version of his character, armor and all. It looked almost like he grabbed the man's soul and ripped it out, tossing it aside.

One person in the crowd took command in an instant fearing that he would have his newly acquired game taken away yelled "ARCHERS AND MAGES FOCUS FIRE ON

HIS HEAD AND FIND WHATEVER WEAK SPOT YOU
CAN!" He bellowed over the silenced crowd. "HEALERS
PICK A WARRIOR AND STICK WITH HIM. WARRIORS
FIND A LEG AND ATTACK IT. STAY CLEAR OF THE
TAIL!" People were stunned at first but began to fall into a
rhythm after a minute or two.

When Zogon's life dropped to fifty percent something
strange happened. A warrior from within the crowd turned
and killed a player behind him. The crowd happened to
have a couple of good frost mages and within an instant he
was frozen from chest to toe, locked in a solid chamber of ice.
"Zogon controlled my mind. There was nothing I could do!"
He screamed.

A fire mage standing nearby released him, "We need all
the tanks we can get."

The warrior smiled, but before he could take another
step three arrows tore through his jugular, "LIAR" an archer
screamed approaching with his bow drawn and aimed at his
head. "Zogon just offered me the same deal. You hear a
whisper; it's soft at first but then grows louder offering you
levels and epic treasures."

After killing the greedy user, the players got back into
their rhythm, dodging Zogon's tail attacks and ignoring his
enticing whispers. At 10 percent Zogon unveiled long golden
glowing wings. The first couple of flaps blew bursts of wind
so strong that it knocked all the surrounding warriors into
the players behind them. Their virtual avatars knocked into
the players behind them, stunning each warrior for a couple
of seconds until their avatar returned.

Once at the ceiling Zogon swooped down targeting an
archer and a healer picking them up like toys as he hurled

them into the air. Their bodies flailed around like rag dolls but before they made impact a bubble froze them in midair. Two mages were now controlling them like puppets, lowering the archer and mage gracefully to the ground. This sent Zogon into a fury, snarling and barking while he sat perched up on a support beam of the arena. The support beam was a good one hundred feet above the ground, too high for almost all of the range attacks. To everyone's surprise he began to devour pieces of steel from the structure scraping at it with his razor sharp claws. It was replenishing his life faster than the hunters long-range shots could drain him.

Once back to fifteen percent life, he snarled, coughing up something fierce from his stomach. His body began to quiver, until a ball of steel came lunging from his throat down onto the users below covered in stomach acids. It killed ten users upon impact, two barely survived by jumping out of the way but the ball of steel rolled onto them crushing their legs. The two crippled users now dragged themselves to the nearest healer screaming for help. Zogon continued to eat metal, vomiting it onto the users below. Hope began to dwindle until a fire mage screamed, "attack the I-beam." Most users were still not used to the game so the idea seemed impossible, but once the fire mage had the structural steel glowing bright red, it began to give way. The I-Beam failed virtually, sending Zogon flailing head first to the ground below. The impact caved in his head sending it into his chest, making it appear like it never existed.

The battle was over. Zogon had killed off at least one hundred and fifty users. Some began to cry and others sat down with frustration. Everyone that died or lived was awarded with VEG gear and a full year of free membership as well as five levels of experience. Also one level 5 epic weapon of your choice was rewarded. The VEG users that survived were elevated to level six and were given a substantial amount of gold. This put even the users that died in a better mood. The crowd was now hugging. You could see the excitement in everyone's eyes, for the first time gamers were interacting in person. The magnitude of VEG hadn't set in but one thing was certain, it was a game changer.

The initial cost for a VEG starter kit was three hundred dollars but the game fee was only fifteen dollars per month. This fee, although some said was expensive, gave you credits towards travel providers like Southwest and Greyhound. VEG ignited the tourism market again. All it took for an abandoned town to thrive again was a single elite boss placed somewhere in its vicinity. People would travel anywhere from around the world if the spoils were rich enough. Monsters roamed the parks, rivers, mountains, and valleys of Earth. VEG allowed gamers to begin interacting in person again. Kids were now seen everywhere outside thrashing their rods at thin air. Clans of fifty to a hundred people would band together to take down bosses on mountaintops to get epic drops and then camp out under the stars to celebrate their victory.

As the game progressed, gamers that were formerly obese and short winded were now physically fit and agile. The prior stereotype of gamers had been erased and now health magazines advertised things like "VEG body workout," or "VEGER shares his secret to rock hard abs" and so on. Cinemas began to incorporate VEG technology, letting players battle the villain in super hero movies after the credits rolled. Before VEG, cinema ticket sales had been on the decline due to pirated movies and torrent downloads. It was much easier to see a movie in the comfort of your own home without having to fight the crowds, plus it was free. People could indulge in movies that they were ashamed to go see at the theatre without being judged. VEG brought theatre sales back to an all-time high, bringing a whole new interactive environment.

Charles Sanders spent a lot of time redesigning the movie experience in general. As a huge fan of choose your own adventure books at a young age, he encouraged most of the major production companies to do the same. You could watch the same movie multiple times and still not see every version of it. During the film, moviegoers could alter the overall outcome. VEG was incorporated into local food markets, home design, as well as professional sports. The world had become an augmented playground and gamers roamed its oceans of code like Indiana Jones hungry for adventure.

In 2020 VEG was in 90 percent of the American households and started to flood the overseas markets. VEG became a part of the average Americans everyday life. In 2022 the government stepped in, deeming the game a distraction. Statistics showed the number of high school dropouts and the neglect of the education system. Charles, knowing the reasoning was sound, installed level caps to ensure that children would strive to finish school. If you didn't graduate from elementary school you couldn't be higher than a level 10 in your character class. If you didn't graduate from middle school then you couldn't get past level 20 and so on. Education was free if people had the drive, and Charles believed that no child should be held back because of their lack of funding. A philanthropist at heart, he donated millions of computers with free lifetime Internet access to children less fortunate. Charles refocused his creativeness upon the school systems, improving the way that teachers taught. He incorporated VEG technology into every classroom. Teachers had access to special architectural software, which would allow them to take a field trip to the Louvre or the Taj Majal by simply creating it in a playground or park. Kids would be walking on the surface of Mars during their science class or digging through Egyptian tombs in World History. Teachers now taught life skills as VEG users were given more experience if they knew how to make fires from scratch as well as understanding how to procure healing remedies. VEG was leading us back to the dream of what humanity could become.

Chapter 2: What Future
Source: Journal
Name: Mark Boggs

I felt claustrophobic in the confines of my room. The bed, washed with neglect, had a thick layer of grey dust on the comforter. I began removing them, along with the pillow covers, hoping that I could sleep through the night without some airborne bacteria taking me. Most hotels in the district had been abandoned when the economic crisis hit. I'm sure the investors in this dump had promising futures that vanished when the markets crashed.

The economic crises changed the fate of many of the restoration city projects. Cash was dumped into slums with hopes of gentrification. When the money train stopped, these cities imploded upon themselves, letting the ghetto swallow them whole. There were still thriving cities in the United States, which is where we focused our development to ensure the economic security of the nation but at the cost of letting some cities die. These abandoned cities were reborn with the funds of black markets and governed by street law. An urban jungle predicated upon the idea that only the fittest would survive.

It was easy for a man like me to find a place to squat when I traveled. VEG had started out as a blessing. No one saw any problems, and get this, even doctors recommended it. I loathed computers. I had always believed that they would be the downfall of mankind. If that damn Charles Sanders would have stayed out of it, I would have been right. VEG changed the world and broke down my preconceived notions of technology.

My daughter got me VEG for my 30th birthday, bless her heart. I might belong in hell for a lot of reasons but being a father isn't one of them. Walking around with my Sally in the recreated version of the city of Atlantis was what did it for me. I became a true believer again. Suddenly there was a light at the end of that bottomless abyss. It was like the hand of God at play, using technology to bring broken relationships crashing back together. VEG gave people purpose, it gave our poor excuse for humanity something it was lacking... hope. I snapped out of thought, finishing the mundane task of stripping the bed.

Ghostels is what they called these hollow shells of former hotels on the street. The higher you climbed the more likely you found a peaceful stay. The homeless and heroin addicts fought like rats over the bottom 5 floors. Without working elevators the climb to the 50th floor would kill them, which is where my room sat. Working water or electricity was something I had come to live without. Sally ran in from the other room and tugged at the sleeve of my wrinkly duffle coat. She loved to play horsy all day and night. If only I had the strength to let her ride forever. I sat down on the bed softly and shook my knee, watching her laugh and scream with joy. I missed these simple moments. It's funny what tasks your body and mind miss.

I was on the case of a rogue user named Gothamsreckoning. A rogue user was one who had pirated a Jacker and jail broke or hacked the software into allowing them free access into VEG. It wasn't unusual and actually more common than one might think. People that freeloaded off the government and my tax bills sickened me. I lit up a cigarette to calm my nerves, blowing clouds of toxic smoke toward the alarm that lay dead upon the cobwebbed ceiling. Sally covered her mouth and began coughing as she made her cute little hand gesture that her mother used to. She covered her nose and wafted her hand in front of it saying "pee yew Daddy." I had quit seven years ago but recently I got the itch. I prayed for cancer to take me every day but no luck. For some reason the lord torments me on this earth and tells me that I'm not done here. Soon though. I'm sure he'll need me soon. I put the cigarette out, creating a mushroom cloud of smoke that engulfed my fist.

The sun was setting in the distance and the light in the room was getting dim. Purples and soft oranges battled on the horizon in a beautiful display. It reminded me of the day my wife left me. I had been drinking again because I couldn't bear the pain. Lindsay was crying in the other room holding a picture in her hands as she quivered, rocking back and forth, back and forth. My vision blurred as I approached, I smelt of anger but I didn't bother to cool. I grabbed the frame as I stumbled into her, seeing the picture sent me into a fury. I smashed it against the wall sending beautiful shards of glass shattering in every direction. I wanted to destroy beauty. I wanted to be an atomic bomb, desolating all life in my wake, letting my void fill with rage. My empty lifeless soul felt something in those moments. I don't remember the rest of the night but I remember that when I woke she was gone. My knuckles bloodied and throbbing. I couldn't have hit her but I wasn't sure.

Sally is now in bed begging for me to read her a story, asking if we can go ride ponies in the morning. I pull out an old beaten up book from her backpack called "The Heroes in My Closet" it's her favorite. It's a scary story of monsters and darkness but every time I read it she tells me bravely that she isn't scared of anything because she has me. By the final page she was sleeping like a baby, leaving me time to do my work.

I slipped on my pads and Jacker and walked out into the hollow screams of the night. I always logged onto VEG while hunting a rogue user because a lot of the time they left hints to their whereabouts in hacked architectural creations. Breadcrumbs so to speak. Police never went that route, which is why they never found rogue users. They believed that if they kicked in enough doors, eventually they would come across one.

The night was colder than most, freezing my eyes in place and drying my throat so that each cough came with spasms of pain. I enjoyed the colder nights. Trashcans filling the alleys, bright with fire, always put a smile on my face. People from all walks of life would gather around them like family to enjoy the warmth. Even the worst turned human for brief fleeting moments helping to stock the fire when it got dim. They all huddled together making sure everyone was close enough to retain the heat.

Street dwellers knew the ins and outs of the slums and were safe among its alleys. I was an outsider, but an armed outsider, so I was equally as safe. The cold muzzle of my Glock 17 rested snuggly on my thigh. I remember how nervous I used to feel when a handgun was holstered on my side. Something in the back of my mind told me that the gun was manufactured wrong and would fire at any moment, sending a bullet piercing through the top of my leg, exiting my foot, crippling me for life. Now I felt I wasn't complete without it. As I walked it shifted back and forth, nuzzling my skin to comfort me on my mission.

The screams increased at midnight, dressing the abandoned alleys with a zombie apocalypse like neglect. The cries were the calls of dead souls grown sick in this decaying wasteland. The gig was simple, wait until an innocent man or woman with a good heart came along to aid the screaming child and reap the spoils. It took advantage of the pure souls left in the world and it usually paid off quite well. I wished this part of the world were a game like VEG but the darkness in life always finds a way to light.

My body stopped dead in its tracks, my ears catching something that sent an alert to my brain. My mind was numb to almost everything so it confused me that it would perk up now. Then I heard it again. This wasn't the scream to trap someone. It was an actual scream of desperation. My legs trembled as I tried to force them to move on and forget it but something inside me had already decided to help. I cursed the gods and turned hard on my heels. I began running in and out of alleyways toward the faint screams echoing from a distant alley.

The stench of alcohol singed the hairs in my nostrils, bringing back memories of pain that danced devilishly in my mind. I had given up drinking a long time ago but now I'd give anything for a swig. Vodka bottles littered the entrance to the alleyway and deep laughter consumed my calm. I could hear the faint whimpers of a little girl. She would be dead if she were any younger than seven... where were her parents? I cringed at the thought of them lying disfigured and lifeless at their daughter's side. I grabbed a broken piece of glass from the vodka bottle next to me and peered around the corner.

Five men were taking turns shoving each other and taking shots of Vodka. All of them had knives except for one, which was waving a chrome snub nose six-shooter in the air wildly in front of a little girl with bruises on both sides of her face. She had been crying for quite some time but her senses seemed like they had begun to dull because she now looked at the man blankly as he yanked her by a clump of her hair. "Tell me where he is and I promise I won't kill you. Look I just want to talk with him." He slapped her coldly across the face with the steel of his six-shooter.

I didn't need to see anything else. I turned the corner and time slowed down. I don't remember pulling my Glock out but it was in my hand perfectly poised and ready to unload when I saw the first one. I took no chances like the action heroes did in movies. My first bullet caved in the head of the only man carrying a gun, probably their leader. His hand stayed locked, grasping the girl's hair as he fell to the ground. I proceeded to shoot two of the others in the chest before I took my first breath. The other two were frozen in place their eyes twitching with fear. I hadn't given their brains time to process the last few actions and now they sat lifeless, replaying the events in their minds like old VCR players. I released two rounds in each of their legs crippling them at the knees.

I approached as death, wrapping the entirety of my hands around the front of their faces, they tried to scream but nothing escaped. Their bodies were weightless in the moment, and I dragged them around the corner. "If you were loved, someone will save you. If not then the streets will claim you." I said coldly as I walked away, heading back toward the limp little girl. I grabbed her underneath the arms and legs and hoisted her up firmly against my chest as I did to Sally when she was a baby. Vomit shot over my shoulder as life sprung back into her. She wept and struggled but I just kept holding her tight. I knew of a safe house not far from my location that had equipment I had hidden incase of emergency. I wouldn't have enough time to track down the rogue user tonight but I had no deadline so this hiccup would only set me back a day or two.

The room was quiet and locked from the inside with decent enough ventilation. Deep fryers, grills, and sinks surrounded where I laid her down. I started a makeshift fire in the oven and rubbed her tiny hands gently between my own blowing life back into them. She looked around thirteen to me with the bruises but then again scars aged anyone. Dark curly black hair tangled and twisted across her caramel colored skin. After a closer look I figured she was eight but I told myself older to make me feel better about her dire situation. She had been sleeping ever since I stuck her with a hit of painkillers. I was lucky a fever hadn't broken out yet.

She wasn't of the streets because she didn't appear sickly like the rest of the abandoned children. She wasn't from upstate because she didn't look plump and pampered. Her muscles were developed and if it weren't for the bruising she would be in good health, a warrior so to speak. She was a little mystery. I began feeling her bones for breaks, checking her up and down meticulously. Her body lay perfectly intact but her cheekbone felt fractured. It gave way a bit when I prodded at it. The symmetry of her face looked fine enough so I decided to bandage it and let it heal naturally.

A lot of people in the US were capable of healing their own wounds because of VEG. The scholastics that Sanders incorporated taught more life skills and survival techniques. If you were a healing class you learned real methods to mend wounds. We learned to work in harmony with the environment around us again. For such a long time we had grown so distant from nature to the point that we feared it. Now we embraced it, even preferred it to staying indoors. Nature used to be a chaos that we couldn't control, its temperature wasn't constant, and therefore it had no order in our minds. We were so use to climate control in our pod environments, having everything ready for us upon arrival. Nature was just a vacation we took, just a couple hours doing something to prove our dominance over it.

The warmth of the fire had now spread through the girl's body, blood flushing back to her face, brightening her cheeks to a rosy red. She nudged her head against my chest just like Sally used to when she was little. "*SALLY!*" my mind screamed at me. This little episode had left my only daughter alone for half the night. The girl's sleep was so deep that she didn't miss a beat in her soft snoring when I picked her up off the ground. After a short walk and a hellish set of stairs I was back to my room on the 50th floor. To my surprise, Sally was sleeping just as deeply as I left her. I placed the injured girl on the other side of the bed, and in no time their chests began to rise and fall in unison. After tucking them in with sanitized sheets from my bag I whispered a lullaby to them that my mother used to sing to me,

"Sleep deep and long my children
Without worry of work or time
Keep and cherish innocence
And always be sublime.

Sleep deep and long my children
Sleep past the darkest day
Keep blind to pain and heartache
Sleep troubled times away.

Sleep deep and long my children
Sleep through all of your regret
Right now sleep for all of us
Have dreams you never forget."

My eyelids fought to stay open, twitching from their battle against sleep. I crawled into bed between them on top of the sheets and fell asleep with their little heads nuzzling against my sides.

I stared at myself in the mirror alternating between full armor and no armor. A Polaroid picture of my former self, taken fifteen years ago, was taped to the lower right hand corner of the mirror. I didn't recognize myself in that photo. I was an obese teenager smiling with sporadic facial hair, holding the BIG AMERICAN FRIED PLATTER, at a county fair. My collared shirt was barely able to tuck into my pants over my enormous belly. Now I stood solid from head to toe, my abs rippling with perfection, a sculpture that the Greeks would have raised proudly.

Pressing the green square button near the center of my rod made my body transform. An oily black battle scorn Spartan helmet masked my cheeks accentuating my eyes. Traditionally the plume was made from coarse horsehairs but mine was lit with a bright red fire that rose a foot above my helm. My chest plate was hardened black steel with white gold rimming my shoulders. My left arm was bare, displaying my sleeve tattoo. It paid homage to the glory days of pixilated graphics. It started with Mario and ended with Guybrush Threapwood, my favorite character from the Monkey Island series, battling Lechuck, the evil villain ghost pirate. My fists were covered with hulk sized black gauntlets. They had a spiral design on the top of each hand, made from glowing gold. The colossal size of them made me appear as a giant in a mere mortal sized body.

I turned my wrists up and down admiring them in the mirror. Then I smiled at my black leggings, seeing the beautiful golden triforce resting just above both of my knees. I had won them in a Zelda quest in Ireland at one of the final castles in an epic battle against Gannon. I pressed the warm circular red button near my trigger finger and my enormous sword manifested itself. It was loosely based off the "Buster sword" that Cloud wielded in Final Fantasy VII and it stood so large that it exited the ceiling of my now seemingly small bathroom. I rested it upon my shoulder and grinned into the mirror.

Tonight my guild was going to raid a PVP castle set up in central park. PVP stood for player verse player. It was almost outlawed if it weren't for the amount of revenue it brought VEG on an annual basis. Since the government took over, lots of what Charles fought against came into play and come to think of it, it was the only reason I supported them. When PVP was first introduced, it was gaming heaven. People created entire concrete arenas for it with beautiful augmented overlays. These bare concrete structures looked bland and ugly to the naked eye but through the Jacker glasses they became other world terrains, medieval castles, or underground caverns on the surface of Jupiter's moon. PVP started out harmless until the first PVP death occurred.

An elite warrior named Nemesis Enforcer (His name probably taken from the original cartoon GI Joe movie) led his clan called Young Bloods into a PVP zone in the Arizona desert. The Young Bloods were comprised of mostly eighteen to thirty year olds with a few exceptions, which were the members that had started the guild. They were a relatively younger group hence their name, but regardless of age they were said to be one of the top clans in the world. The challenging clan came from the northeast and were called the Spartans. They were known for their formations and the fact that no matter what army they approached they would always bring a smaller force to battle. What they lacked in numbers they made up with in skill. Their leader was a dual wielding warrior named Leonidas. PVP was exciting because once a player was killed he was not allowed to enter anything VEG related for seven days. That rule made it so that battles wouldn't last forever especially since reviving in the arena was banned.

The battle lasted for four days. On the fourth and final day Nemesis Enforcer stood against Leonidas for a final push. Both armies had lost all but around twenty players, most being healers and DPS that were still alive. They were casting buffs on their leaders as they slashed at each other again and again.

Nemeses Enforcer had lost one of his key healers in the final moments of the battle and the tide began to turn into the hands of the Spartans. In a sole act of desperation Nemeses Enforcer lunged at Leonidas, his right fist making contact with the center of his face caving in his nose. Blood began to pour from Leonidas's collapsed nostrils. The other players stopped in disbelief as Nemeses Enforcer tackled Leonidas to the ground whaling his fists with murderous intent. Leonidas struggled to defend the murderous blows at first, his arms flailing at his sides until his screams slowed and stopped, turning to soft gurgles. Nemeses Enforcer then regained his footing and destroyed what was left of the Spartans army, which had begun to scatter.

The creators hadn't accounted for any kind of physical ramifications. With the user unconscious or dead one could easily destroy their character still logged in. Through a loophole in the system, Nemeses Enforcer finished Leonidas off and claimed victory as his teammates stood silent. Shortly after, the police arrived on the scene to arrest Bobby Sparks aka Nemeses Enforcer while paramedics tried to save the life of Brandon Miller a twenty eight year old law student from Ohio. He died before he reached the nearest hospital. News stories ran rampant across the nation.

Charles banned PVP and installed new programming that would banish your character the second that physical contact was made. The game footage would be reviewed and if they deemed the contact non aggressive then you were given back full access. The government stepped in, saying the decision was made with haste and reinstated PVP after the rules had been revamped proving once more who had true control of the game.

My office collapsed upon itself on nights like this, to where only I existed, my own perfect automated environment of which I controlled every aspect. My chair set to lean only three inches from its upright position, raised exactly five inches from its base. The A/C scheduled to cool to an icy sixty-seven degrees Fahrenheit from eight PM to ten o'clock, and then heat back up to a cool seventy at midnight. My fitted suit, precisely cut to complement my slim physique accented by my power tie, that's tip touched the top of my silver belt buckle. My desk, designed in the most optimum way for efficiency, had zero clutter.

The only item that seemed out of place was my picture frame, with black trim edges to match my glossy black desk. It was meant to keep me looking normal in the eyes of my superiors, whose visits were rare. Merit wasn't enough for the bunnies that hopped from office to office, leaving pellets of crap that lingered for hours. No, these sick individuals needed to see that you were a "family man," to feel comfortable in your presence. Since I myself was not the "family type," my sickening attempt at humoring the masses was of my childhood. It was my family in front of a stereotypical suburban home. Mom and Dad stood with bright smiles plastered on their faces, my father's right hand resting on my shoulder. Cliffy, my German Shepherd, was sitting upright next to me, her head almost the same height as mine. Her tongue wet, dripping with saliva, making me shutter as I studied it now. I don't know why I chose this picture out of the hundred others, probably because people related with animal lovers. Cliffy was put down shortly after that photo. What the photo didn't show was that Cliffy was a female and pregnant. I remember loving the dog more than anything when I was younger until that one day.

Cliffy had just given birth to four pups and was now licking her enflamed private areas. The garage smelt musty and was too hot for my liking but the idea of an animal giving birth intrigued me. I went in, against my father's wishes, knowing that Cliffy would do nothing to hurt me. Her eyes were tired with the labors of birth; she was letting out long sighs followed by short whimpers. *Stay away from her son, dogs are funny right after they give birth. It stirs up some kind of protective instinct*, I heard my dad's voice echoing in my mind. I wanted to get a look at my new friends though, so I crawled in closer. The air settled thick, so thick that I could feel it heavy upon my skin like water resisting each inch closer. Then it felt like fog clearing, I could see their cute little innocent faces letting out shrill high pitched squeals. Warmth covered me, the environment making me feel like I was just being born to her as well. I got closer wanting now to lie next to them and then it happened. It was three quick snap shots. The first was of me full of life and wonder taken from a couple feet away, embracing the entire scene. The second was a close up of Cliffy's pearly white teeth sunk deep into my right arm. Blood oozing out slow, thick and dark like molasses. The third was someone different, someone changed, a version of my prior self that I didn't recognize. A dark void of misunderstanding, doubt, and shame all brewing inside. The photos were only flashes I saw, a dream or a memory I couldn't tell, before I blacked out.

I woke up in a hospital, my mother crying by my side. She came in close when my eyes fluttered, but I pushed her away. Her touch sickened me, as did my weakness. I asked her where the bitch was. I specifically referred to her as a bitch instead of Cliffy. My parents took note and looked at me in disbelief.

They let me rest longer, but when it came time to come home I wouldn't take a step in the house. It felt tainted, even unsafe for the first time. My parents made Cliffy wear a muzzle but I still felt it, somewhere in the back of my mind a fear lurked gripping my every action, listening to my every word. Within three days I had them put Cliffy down. The life fading from her eyes was a curious sight. It was like a syringe drawing out her soul, slow and coldly calculated, and at the same time injecting me with life. I felt almost godlike. I asked if they could bring her back now, and my parents only cried thinking I didn't understand death and that I chose to put her down prematurely. It wasn't that at all. I wanted to revive her and kill her all over again except I wanted the needle.

I snapped back to the present when a light knock disrupted the sleep of my door. The knock of the soulless cowards that roamed my floor, likely an over privileged intern whose Daddy got them a job to play political activist for the year. Just another notch on their puke packed resume. I waited, holding my breath and hoping this one wouldn't have the balls to knock again, but then it came, another whisper of a knock. "COME IN," I shouted in a commanding tone, as to scare the piss out of whoever it was. The door peaked open just enough for John, a junior level analyst, to stick his nose in. I didn't mind John because he kept to himself and had a solid work ethic. He never joined in with the others jolly routine and looked almost uncomfortable when someone tried to socialize with him during work hours.

It baffled me how some of the fucking parasites in this office would stand next to John's desk, only when they had no one else to talk to as if he were a last resort to delay their days work. They would try and force awkward conversation on him even if he was obviously busy. Standing there with an insincere tone asking asinine questions that they didn't care to know the answers to.

"John, come in." I said. The young man stumbled inside and his stammer made me smile a bit.

"I, I got the results you were looking for sir."

"Go on." I had only asked him an hour ago, the boy worked quick.

"In three months the town saw triple its profits across the board."

"Excellent work John. That will be all." The door shut respectfully soft and my controlled environment reverted to normal.

My mind danced delightfully to the news to some sort of jazzy Frank Sinatra tune. Still there was that fear lurking like a snake underneath my collar closing around my necktie, squeezing at my throat, infecting my thoughts with torturous venom. *They are coming for you, they own you and your pathetic job. You call this a day's work? You think you have power? They own three quarters of the global market and could destroy this disgusting excuse for an economy with the flick of a finger. Admit it, you coward. The Chinese will take over the world and you will be left with the pups begging for a fucking morsel.* I slammed my fist against my chest forcing the breath I had been holding in screaming out as I gasped for air. The panic hit me more often these nights. I shot out an e-mail to inform my superiors of John's findings, packed up my laptop to call it a night.

The hour was late and the only lit establishments were pizza joints and fast food Chinese. My stomach growled at me like some sort of alien entity. The Chinese restaurant on 52nd street danced in my mind. It would be nice to sit amongst the cockroaches that plagued this planet. The idea of ordering an obscene amount of food and disposing of most of it in front of malnourished servants scrounging by intrigued me.

The décor was overloaded with bright reds and those trendy paper lanterns that invaded your eating space. I sat at a table near the back where I wouldn't be bothered by customers looking for late night conversations. When the waitress came I snatched the menu from her hands and motioned for her to leave at once. She gave a semi-formal submissive bow and walked away keeping an eye on me until I had decided.

After ten minutes or so I threw a single look in her direction and she came scurrying over like a pitiful dog waiting on its master. When she fumbled for her pen and paper I gave her a sharp piercing glare, until she apologized and placed it back in her hip apron. I then proceeded to order as many things as I could on the menu knowing I would only be able to stomach an eighth of the amount.

After thirty minutes my food came pouring out of the kitchen. The woman had to make two separate trips to get it all. I inspected every item and that's when I snapped. I would not come to know that the woman was Thai, *I hated the Chinese*. I would not come to find that she had willfully entered herself into a black market mail order bride outfit to find refuge and a better future for her and her two-year-old daughter, **I hated the Chinese**. I never cared to ask about the bruise on her face that she received from her abusive American husband, *I HATED THE CHINESE*. I would never know her struggle, sneaking out every weekday while her husband was at work, to a minimum wage shit job, just to save up enough money for her and her daughter to escape, **I HATED THE CHINESE**. I would not be a part of the investigation team that would find a Thai woman and her four-year-old daughter with blunt force trauma to the right and left temples, lying dead near a riverbank, **I HATED THE FUCKING CHINESE**. My Wonton soup came out as sweet and sour with a black hair in it, and this Chinese bitch was responsible. The manager assured me that she would never work in their establishment again once I mentioned my employer. I hadn't eaten a bite yet my stomach now felt content.

I walked back toward my apartment building, which was located across the street from my work. The porter held the door open nodding to me as I entered, knowing that the mundane formalities bothered me. I glided past him as if he were an inanimate object. On my way to the elevator, the buzzing of my pocket interrupted my stride. My cell phone slid unrestricted out of my pants and I looked in shock at the caller ID. Sector 8 lit up brightly as the phone shook my hand, I answered and said, "two minutes" and then hung up the phone.

I darted into the elevator, inserted my key while hitting the 61st floor button and a moment later I was zooming up to my rooftop penthouse apartment. I got off before the doors could finish opening and ran toward the only door on the floor that read fifty-one overtop. I could hear the soft click of the door remotely unlocking as it read the keys in my pocket. I pushed and I was home. Dim lights filled my apartment and I took out my cell phone saying, "Call back."

My phone did all the rest. I put the warm receiver against my frozen ear and listened.

"Commence operation black out." Then the phone went dead. A smile started somewhere deep within me, creeping through my body to the right and left sides of my face, tugging at my lips. I dropped my phone to my side, feeling the power engulf me. It was time.

Chapter 5: Blackout
Source: NEWS BROADCAST LIVE

Debra Conners: "That is fascinating Tom, So you're telling me that scientists will now be able to inform parents just two months after conceiving whether or not their child will be attracted to the same sex with a simple in vitro test?"

Tom Rinton: "That's correct Debra, a year ago we discovered the gene that causes homosexuality and it has been just a matter of researching and producing an affordable test to screen for it. Now parents will be able to prepare for their child's sexual orientation beforehand giving their child a more encouraging environment."

Debra Conners: "I have been reading so much about this lately, I think the first question on everyone's mind is whether or not scientists would be able to tamper with this gene?"

Tom Rinton: "No Debra, we will only be able to test for it."

Debra Conners: "Well Tom, I really appreciate your time."

Tom Rinton: "Thank you for having me."

Debra Conners: "In other news the vote on abortion has radically changed from pro-life to pro-choice. We will be taking a poll on whether these recent findings from Tom Rinton had anything to do with it. You decide, but right now we will go to George Timpton with breaking news on the revolutionary game VEG."

George Timpton: "Thank you Debra. We are here in front of

the VEG headquarters in New York City, where just now VEG announced that a group of hackers led by the notorious Gothamsreckoning infiltrated the systems code and shut down the entire country of China. It is unknown how they accomplished such a feat but VEG spokesman Wally Dandor has assured us that VEG programmers are working around the clock to reinstate the countries access to the globally popular game. What this means is that China has become a dead zone with nothing to offer for VEG users until the programming has been fixed. China has been very patient and said that they will combine efforts to help get VEG back online in their country. Back to you Debra."

END OF BROADCAST

Chapter 6: Keep Your Eyes Open
Source: Blog

THE TERRIBLE TRUTH

The End Is Near

Last Wednesday, March 31st at 1700 hours, Charles Sanders, the creator of VEG, was found dead at his residence in Wolfeboro, New Hampshire. He had become a hermit since his wife passed away fifteen years ago during the birth of their first and only child. Neither the child nor his wife survived. I wish I could say that his death came as a surprise but I know our government all too well.

Let me give you all a little background on VEG for the new readers. VEG, simply put, is an economic powerhouse. Inserting a boss or mob with the chance for a rare artifact or epic drop in any rural location is like creating Disney World in the town's backyard. VEG users will travel by the thousands to complete these quests and stay for however long is needed, spending money on local services and in doing so driving up the local economy.

Once the government realized VEG's power and potential they took control. The easiest way to do so was by riding in on the back of our own democracy. Smoke and mirrors people, smoke and mirrors and before we knew it we voted in favor of a hostile takeover. The kicker is that they made it appear like it was our idea. News broadcasts infiltrated our homes and minds with bullshit statistics, showing how VEG destroyed the education of our precious youth. What does this great man Charles Sanders do when he hears the statistics? Like any great man he goes to focusing all his efforts into our horrific education system making it the most prestigious system in the world. Now, parents from Europe and Asia are sending their kids to America as young as eleven years old. The terrible truth all along was that the amount of dropouts was the same before and after VEG.

Let's look at the statistics, since we all love statistics so much. After just fifteen years from VEG's launch, ninety percent of our children have become bilingual and ninety five percent have reading levels that exceeded their age by an average of two years. Charles was more conscientious of the American schooling system than our government has ever been. The same government that made cuts year after year to our education system all of the sudden decided that Charles Sanders was ruining our youth. Threaten a child's future and the parents will not rely on logic to make their decision. It was genius, and we took the bait hook, line, and sinker. We voted for the government's involvement and ownership rights of VEG and once they took control it was only a matter of time. Monthly fees increased but were justified by the glorified new statistics of how our precious youth was doing. Our children were safe and the fees and new rules were only a side note. The ownership rights by the time Charles's wife was pregnant had fallen almost entirely under governmental control. Charles did his part and put up the good fight but after the first PVP death he lost all accountability in the eyes of the American people. It was then that Charles locked himself away for the second time in his New Hampshire home fearing for his own life. His fight was diminishing and he spent most of his time trying to give back to charities. He was broken, a man trying to live out the rest of his days in peace. That is how he died, a great man hated by the people he tried so desperately to save.

The burial service for Charles was one that has been unsurpassed by any public figure in the last decade. He is the first person to have ever been buried in Central Park, New York. A statue, built by an unknown artist, was placed behind his grave. It displayed Charles Sanders in his youth, standing in front of a treasure chest shaped like the earth. His pose was that of one in thought. Around his neck, is a key that's end didn't fit the globe's lock. Without using VEG the statue is an astonishing sight, but when viewed through the Jackers it truly comes to life.

It shows a scene of Charles Sander's soul being sucked from his body, manifesting itself in front of the chest. His physical body collapses on the ground but the key from his neck stays levitating. Then his visage swirls in midair twisting and twirling with the key until they bind together floating into the keyhole, opening the chest that he couldn't unlock in his lifetime. When the chest opens a high contrasted light shoots up into the heavens, beautiful pastel colors dance around its outskirts shooting off wisps of gold in every direction.

When VEG players place their hand inside the light, it removes their armor and reveals their true skin. I'd like to think that the statue resembles the fact that Charles Sanders gave his life for our happiness and the unity that he hoped he would accomplish in life would hopefully follow his death.

The service took place on Sunday with thousands of VEG players from around the world pouring into the park to gather around his grave. After a few simple words in the Eulogy an extraordinary act occurred. A group of five people in the front row, believed to be close friends of Charles, all knelt on one knee with their right hand in a fist on the ground and their left hand bent in towards their chest touching their hearts as they hung their heads. It was a tradition that started among the first VEG users. They were a part of Charles Sanders clan when VEG was created. They did it to show fealty as a warrior would on the battlefield when his general would perform the accolade ceremony. A promise that they would carry on his vision of VEG to unite the world. It started as a kind of joke among his colleagues but then became a tradition. After Charles had stopped playing VEG the ritual hadn't been performed or seen in over a decade. Like a wave, the entire crowd kneeled in turn. No words were shared; just a silent promise was made that filled the hearts of every person that attended, a promise that we would all continue his legacy.

Charles stood for everything we hope for in this country. He was a man that should have been President of the United States and now has been vanquished by a sect in our own government. I know one thing for certain; Charles Sanders was murdered. This might be my last blog post and if it is I'd like to share with you the whole terrible truth and not the smoke screen they want you to see. The reason that Charles Sanders became a hermit is because he feared for his own life. I have reason to believe that he was threatened by the government before and he didn't concede, which led to his wife and unborn child's death. The fact that he stayed alive for so long after their death is the only part of this story I didn't expect. The government must be planning something big that would require the elimination of Charles Sanders. Though they have working knowledge of VEG's source code, they are still infantile when it comes to what Charles Sanders knows. Keep your eyes open children and you will see their plan come to fruition shortly. When that time comes, rise up like Charles Sanders did and fight the good fight for the soul of this country, because right now it's almost gone… and that my friends is the Terrible Truth.

Chapter 7: Awake Now Mark Boggs
Source: Journal
Name: Mark Boggs

I awoke with a jolt, remembering the prior night's events. A slight dip in the bed lay vacant by my side. The little girl had slipped away in the night. That had never happened to me and I smiled at how tired I must have been. "C'est la vie," I said out loud as I bounced up off the bed.

It was already noon, I must have gotten back late last night. I didn't feel comfortable hunting during the day but I had lost time saving the girl. I made myself a hearty lunch and watched as Sally ate her food. She liked to cut it up into the smallest bits. I would always tell her that if she made it too small ants would come and take it away. It never failed to put a smile on her face and she would begin to eat her food.

The streets were barren, forgotten under the afternoon sun. The hustle and bustle of anyone stuck working in the district was gone before the sunset. A new breed awakened at night, crawling out from all the foul places parents warned their children about. I had been tracking Gothamsreckoning for close to four years now and he had been eluding me thus far. This transient scumbag never stayed put. Days turned to weeks, and weeks bled into years. I had been searching VEG spikes, an excessive amount of server usage recorded by a single user. I scoured the slums looking for abnormal activity. Gothamsreckoning was a big fish and the payout for his capture would set me up for life. It was more than that though, some illusive obsession that tugged at lost memories.

I walked past the same alley where I had diverted my path the prior night, putting on my Jackers to begin the hunt. The first couple of streets showed little promise, barren wastelands void of both life and atmosphere. The sun was starting to set and shadows began creeping up abandoned alleys, filling them with their familiar gloom. I dove deeper into the maze, looking for any modified buildings and that's when I saw it. I turned a corner and a new world stood before my eyes. I recognized it... Virtual rain fell thick, soaking neon lit alleys. Police cars hovered above head whipping fog filled streets into momentary chaos.

Rogue users seemed to gravitate toward the science fiction genre, leaving breadcrumbs for the truly dedicated fans. I had studied countless science fiction films. My favorite of which was Blade Runner and now I was immersed in its world. Gothamsreckoning must have recreated a sci-fi haven where he felt at home. I was standing in awe of its intricate beauty.

It was hard to tell what was augmented reality and what was physically standing before me. I turned one of my lenses on my Jackers off so I could differentiate between the two. Most of the city disappeared in my left eye, just a few people walking aimlessly in the distance. I could see the Tyrell Corporation's two-pyramid skyscraper engulfing the horizon. In the film, Tyrell was a high-tech corporation that made androids. Their company motto was, "more human than human." The problem being that they made replicants, non-human bioengineered beings that became illegal on earth due to an off-world mutiny. Six replicants from the tragic event escaped, stealing a shuttle to Earth.

Zhora, one of the replicants from the mutiny, was running in my peripheral with her clear plastic raincoat on.

A doe, attempting escape in front of black market knock off clothing stores. Rick Deckard, a cop hunting replicants played by Harrison Ford, was in pursuit. His gun was drawn and poised. She began crashing through store windows after he released a bullet that pierced through her right shoulder. Brilliant shards of virtual glass danced with gravity, reflecting lights into the mannequin's emotionless eyes. It was such a beautiful scene up close. She regained her footing, trying desperately to keep running but she was more frantic than before, fear flooding her enlarged pupils. Another bullet tore through her chest sending her diving face first into the ground. She was now just as dead and lifeless as the mannequins that stood beside her in the storefront window.

It made sense to have her die next to hollow human forms since she was a replicant. At the time of her death, Deckard felt that replicants were nothing more than soulless robots. I examined the body but something looked different. I brought up a virtual display in my Jackers of the exact same scene from Blade Runner. Yes!!... her body was different. Her fingers were all flat in the original scene, sprawling out like she had tensed up upon death. In this version, her right hand was above her head with the palm facing upward. I looked toward the same direction and saw nothing. The buildings looked identical to the original film. I looked again at the palm of her hand, it appeared as though it was awaiting an offering. Something strange grabbed my memory, laying waste to control. I pulled a piece of paper from my pocket and began to fold and crease like a mad man. My possessed fingers lost themselves in a daze of origami. When I came to, a delicate white paper unicorn was nuzzled amongst the hardened cracks of my ogreish hands. The unicorn represented a theory that Deckard was in fact himself a replicant. I placed it in her hand. The earth paused and her polished fingers closed upon it. An almost blinding light flashed above. On top of the building was the Chinese symbol for origin. Ridley Scott, the director, placed these symbols throughout the movie. My heart raced knowing that it was probably a clue. I pulled out my Glock 17 and approached the front entrance.

It was dark inside, the kind of dark that masked bravery, so I clipped a flashlight mod onto my pistol. Times like these, I felt I was back in the Army. The collection agency job kept me grounded. The only flash of purpose since retiring from the Green Beret. It made the pain I felt constructive, and missions gave me purpose. They never tell you how hard it'll be to try and be a family man after you've watched kids die in your arms. Life feels like a dark dream you once had. After the wife left the nightmares took me most nights, seething with despair. The collection agency brought back some normality, the muscle memory trigger responses kept me focused. I lived for the case, lived almost too much for this one.

My light bounced down long corridors revealing eroded life as I searched. The number of stairs I had climbed made me dizzy, doors began to blend together. Opened or closed they all reeked of neglect. Another stair set, another step toward the inevitable truth that I had found another dead end. Nothing, there was nothing, nothingness plagued my pupils into a trance, making the mind tired. Floor thirteen... floor fourteen... Floor fifteen... floor sixteen... Wait floor sixteen. My left eye saw a vacant corridor like the others but my right eye saw the rooftop in one of the final scenes in Blade Runner. Smog from the ventilation cascaded over dull metal covering the neon lit letters TDK, one of the many corporate ads of companies that didn't succeed after the movie other than Coke. Rain bounced so realistically off the sleeves of my coat that I instinctively attempted to brush it away. I caught myself shivering, the impulse ingrained in my brain.

Roy Batty, another replicant, was already sitting cross-legged like a child, his head wavering a little with blood running from a cut around his left eye. He spoke, "I've seen things you people wouldn't believe. Attack ships on fire off the shoulder of Orion. I watched C-beams glitter in the dark........."

It was beautiful, but my focus was distracted by something. Above one of the doors further down the hall there was some sort of beautiful glittering light in the sky. Curiosity drew me in for a closer look but I saw nothing. I waited for about fifteen minutes for the loop of the speech to reset. Then I stood near the area that I thought I saw it. Mid speech I saw it, a borage of lasers, which I imagine represented C-beams, battled above the crown molding. The bronze apartment number sixteen fifty-two shimmered in the spectacle. A small insignia GR was carved into the wood frame just above the numbering.

Gothamsreckoning.... An ecstasy type feeling flooded my veins as adrenaline carried me to the door, my body shaking with the anticipation of my first kick. My busy mind rested and took audience for the physical performance to come. The smash rang in my ears, a symphony of raw pleasure, as my army reinforced steel-toed boot unleashed at full force near the doorknob. I had already calculated the force required, given the age of the dilapidated structure, and applied four hundred percent over just for sheer effect. It tore from the bottom first, ripping from its hinges. Then the swinging force sent the door airborne, twisting in the air like a propeller. It crashed into a table in the center of the room as I ran in gun drawn.

The soft click of a trip wire whispered hello in my ears. I didn't even feel it, my body froze knowing it was too late to react. The entire floor shot up around me, trapping me in a thin mesh netting. My senses were sharp enough to know to log off from VEG. The net material was made of metal so I knew I had mere seconds. If a person stayed logged on, hackers could access anything and everything in their life. VEG technology had taken the place of cellphones and computers because it incorporated them all into one. I said "Sally," my code to activate my automatic shutdown, and the VEG simulation went blank locking just before the pulse of electricity knocked me unconscious.

Chapter 8: The Match
Time: Six Years Prior
Source: Personal Computer Log
User: Evo

The cold air nipped at my exposed left arm. I wore clothing that mimicked my characters skins, so it left my arm exposed to show off my pixilated tattoo. Skins were augmented gear that you picked up by questing, PvP, looting bosses, or drops off killing random creeps. It was like a new pair of virtual clothing to show off to other users. Each item made your character stronger or weaker depending on what kind of character build you wanted to specialize in.

One could wear heavy suited armor for tanking. Most tanks do little damage to others but can stay alive forever with the right healers. Tank characters, such as warriors, are meant to run in and take the brunt of the attacks so that the weaker players may stay alive. I didn't like the defensive build, due to the fact that it was monotonous. So, I went with lighter armor, leaving myself with little defense. It made me more of an offensive killing machine. My character build maximized chances for critical hits giving double the damage with a single blow. This also gave me higher probability to bash and stun my enemy leaving them susceptible to all sorts of attacks. I was agile for a warrior and almost felt like a rogue.

A lot of people asked why I didn't go for the rogue class. I didn't take to the rogue because they had too little health. In prior video games, rogues could go invisible allowing them to come in close for a surprise attacks. In VEG everyone can see you so, without the element of surprise I ranked rogues around the level of useless. Lots of others would argue their case. Gamers would defend their class by developing outside the box strategies while watching PvP replay footage in a foul smelling basement. Tricks only lasted for so long though and were countered within a day or two.

A single file line was gathering at the south entrance of Central Park where my guild was scheduled to meet. Gatekeepers with scanners sat at the north, east, south, and west entrances. Gatekeepers were rule police / administrators. They wore riot gear and helmets that masked their identity. Their helmets reminded me of a cross between Daft Punk and Cobra Commander's headpieces. It was meant to conceal their identity from disgruntled players. To be able to fight in PvP you had to be scanned by a Gatekeeper to access the arena. If you didn't get scanned your player would be banned once you walked into the park during PvP hours. VEG users had been working for years on how to hack or bypass the barriers to PvP arenas without success. You could still get hacked armor and swords past the PvP barriers but illegal entrance was impossible.

I met up with Kira, Knightcr@wler, and Phantom upon arrival. They were the usual crew that I ran missions with.

"What's up Evo," Phantom said while shaking my hand and hugging me.

My full user name was .iIi.Evolution but people called me Evo for short. The symbol ".iIi." was what I felt resembled the evolution of man. We had started as animals, evolved to a certain point, then began our decline. That was until VEG appeared. I had used that name though in the days of console and computer gaming and it had kind of stuck. I gave everyone a quick hug. "Ready to ride once more my brothas?" They all smiled. I felt comfortable with these guys and we had become close friends over our years of questing.

Kira, the only female in our group, was tall and slender with long black hair. On PvP days she wrapped it up in a bun, otherwise she said that it got in her way. Being half Japanese and half American earned her the nickname Half Jap which she received when a song came on the radio by Weezer where the first lyrics said "God damn you half Japanese girls".

Kira was one of the best healers in our clan. She used a Spirit Mage as her class. Spirit Mages called upon nature's spirits to heal the living. She had a high damage per second build (DPS) for PvP, which catches a lot of users off guard. She could switch skins at the drop of a hat, which allowed her to play both defensive and aggressive. Her armor she currently had equipped was a beautiful pink and purple robe that draped behind her feet when she walked. She wielded a long golden staff with a miniature phoenix trapped inside a glowing red orb at the tip. Her phoenix had a yearlong cool down period. That meant that once summoned, you would have to wait a year before you could use it again. It was only used if we were in a dire situation. Various glowing rings covered her fingers and both her wrists were lined with different golden bangles. She had beautiful blue eyes that stood out from her creamy beige skin.

The second member in our group was Knightcr@wler who played a speed knight. The speed knights were one of the original classes of VEG and one of Charles's favorites. Most classes were given bonuses for physical movement but the speed knights relied on their natural speed to be able to do the most damage. Charles had incorporated these bonuses to encourage our country to get back into physical shape. We all joked about how if VEG hadn't taken over Knightcr@wler's life that he would have won an Olympic gold by now. It was most likely true; he was the fastest person I had ever seen. He had a runner's physique and only at his top speeds was he a brilliant player to watch. The faster a Speed Knight could run the more damage he would build up on a single blow. If he reached a certain sustained speed, he was given more options for devastating attacks and spells.

Knightcr@wler and two other people in the US could reach a speed that would allow them to unleash the deadly apocalyptic fury. The apocalyptic fury spell stunned every player within thirty feet of the knight, draining half his or her life no matter what class. The target of the spell would either end up dead or on the verge of death. It was argued that the spell was unfair, but then again, only a few people could reach the speed required to cast it. Many users had tried to use cars, bicycles, and mopeds to trick the system into thinking they had acquired the speed it took but it never worked. One had to reach the speed themselves with their own two legs. The best part about the speed that Knightcr@wler could attain was that he could cast another spell that made him invulnerable upon retreat. This gave him a good ten seconds to escape as long as he maintained his momentum.

The speed knight was also given buffs and bonuses the faster he or she moved while attacking. You had to be agile and have an incredible amount of stamina to be elite with the class. Knightcr@wler was number one in the US and I was happy to have him by my side.

Our final team member Phantom was an Assassin. Assassins are great for ranged attacks or close hand to hand combat. His had a range build where he would load up DPS on characters we were attacking. It didn't take someone that skilled to be an assassin but Phantom was good, plus we all liked his personality. He was quick witted and provided a good laugh from time to time.

Our clan leader's name was Kenshin, which was fitting because he played an undead samurai. He was standing next to the gatekeeper and ushering us in one by one. "Everyone meet by the Hallett Nature Sanctuary and we will discuss strategy," he called out as the group filed through the gate.

We were all part of the clan called Pure Pwnage after one of our favorite Canadian TV shows. Pure Pwnage was a comedy about pro gamers, need I say more. It attracted almost everyone I knew to the group. Even one of the characters, FPS Doug from the show, was in our guild but no one ever got to play with him because he rarely came down south to raid or PvP with us.

Once gathered, Kenshin informed our clan that the other team's castle was located in Sheep Meadows. It was a wide-open grassy field that would most likely have a makeshift castle made out of scaffolding and temporary walls. Kenshin had given our group of four a separate mission from the main clan. We were ordered to scout the grounds and to kill any stragglers. Also, we were tasked to try and find another way into the castle. We took off at once at a light jog; our speed would increase once we had Sheep Meadows in sight.

I felt a chill run through my spine, climbing from the base, making my fingers tingle. I was always a bit nervous no matter how much confidence I had in my crew. The castle came into view in the distance and our jog increased into a sprint. We cut along the tree line on the outskirts of the clearing. We had almost gotten to the western edge of the castle when Phantom stopped dead in his tracks. He was gifted as an assassin and had the ability to perceive bad events before they occurred. Kira grabbed me by the shoulder pulling me down to the ground. Knightcr@wler fell in behind us. Not more than one hundred yards was a group of a hundred crouched enemy users. Luck was with us because they were too busy starring at the clearing to notice us. It was a group set to flank our main from the east.

Communication was cut off from our army because of a standard area of effect spell that had been cast by the enemy. It made it so that any message over ten feet would be rejected. There would be no way to warn our approaching army that was still a good fifteen minutes out. Attempting a retreat would compromise our position. The distance was also too short for Knightcr@wler to build up speed for the appropriate amount of time to perform his deadly apocalyptic fury. We had to act though, knowing that a flanking group of this size could destroy our army.

Knightcr@wler crouched low beneath the brush and began moving his fingers furiously in midair. He looked like an idiot savant composing Mozart to deafening silence. A message appeared suspended in front of us saying the following:

Knightcr@wler · *Can't pick up enough sustained speed from this distance to have a chance to take them. If I backtrack I could be seen.*

We all sat in silence then another message appeared from Kira. Kira – *In ten seconds run at them I will make you a path, then attack at their rear.*

Kira then moved her rod in a circular motion as if practicing Tai Chi. Her rod twirled in her hand as she chanted French words that sounded like lyrics to a love song.

Charles incorporated a unique language for each class. Spirit Mages used French to cast spells and summons; Assassins spoke Arabic; Warriors used Old Norse; Speed Knights revived Latin. Because of this, we were all fluent in at least a second language if not a third. Kira was fluent in English, Japanese, and French. One of my favorite parts of VEG was that it had revived dead languages. Some people even studied Egyptian hieroglyphics for quests. VEG encouraged education and rewarded intellect with rare treasures. The more knowledge a user had, the more useful they were to a group, and the better equipment they could attain. Charles wanted to bring America back from its slumber. He wanted all children to be bilingual like most other countries in the world and it worked.

Kira was standing up now with her head tilted downwards, her words once curing turned quick to poison spewing from her venomous lips. We could hear some yelling in the distance. Before I could locate the source, Knightcr@wler was already sprinting at full speed, darting in and out of trees as to evade line of sight attacks. Through our Jackers, we could see white streams streaking behind him, his character resembling the wind. Kira, in one fluid motion, brought her hands crashing together and an enormous beam of white light was unleashed from her staff. *Of course, a damage over time ray*, I thought. Damage over time spells did more and more damage the longer one stayed in the line of fire.

The entire army was bunched together. If they decided to stay, by the time Knightcr@wler got to their location they would all be drained by at least a third of their life. If they decided to flee they would give Knightcr@wler the running room he needed to release his devastating attack. It was working; they began to scatter, running to evade the now blinding focus beam. Knightcr@wler ran right into the center of Kira's spell, to where his blur of speed and her light beam became one.

Kira was now shouting French words, strengthening the beam into a white-hot fury. I didn't even think about the fact that our healer was now attacking, leaving Knightcr@wler completely vulnerable. He would need help if he wanted to have any chance of making it to the rear of their group alive. Phantom and I must have realized it at the same time because we both jumped up and began using all our buffs on Knightcr@wler, who was barely within range. I cast my warrior's protection bubble, which had a monthly cool down. It would leave me pretty defenseless but I knew that this could be the act that won the battle.

The enemy users were fleeing in every direction from the focus beam. The ones that had fled too far to the east had placed themselves on open grounds and Phantom was shooting to kill with a hunter's accuracy. Knightcr@wler went through them in a flash and then it happened, we saw the wake of a nuclear blast shoot ripples across the erupting ground. A mushroom cloud shot up into the sky rocketing at the hunter's full moon. A simple matter of cleanup was in order with a couple area of effect spells and the entire army was dead. We all came out unscathed, cheering as we watched the army leave to the west gate. Once dead, you were automatically instructed to exit to the nearest gate. If a player took steps the opposite direction of an exit, they would automatically be disqualified from arena fights for two months. Communication links were terminated and VEG access was denied.

The caster of the communication spell must have been within the group that we just slaughtered because messages were now getting through to Kenshin. Our clan linked to our chat about the flanking army to the east's eradication. Text cheers poured in, filling up our vision like a virus. The battle was looking to be in our favor.

We rendezvoused at the front of the castle, thinking that they were close to surrendering. We knew we were wrong when we heard the roar. An enormous black dragon summon clawed its way free of the castle walls, screaming into the night's sky. I had never seen one, but had heard of them. The quest to receive the summon was near impossible, because it required enough money to travel around the world twice.

We could hear cheers hailing from the interior castle walls. It irked the hell out of me and I felt my temper rising from somewhere dark inside. The place where sick sadistic thoughts brewed, yet never emerged. Those cold chilling visions of kicking a cute puppy, pushing your friend in front of a car, or stabbing someone with a serving knife at Thanksgiving dinner. Momentary lapses of insanity that lay dormant within the mind. I smiled thinking of one that very moment and calmed my mind to focus on strategy.

We didn't need to warn Kenshin about a possible ambush from the west because he had already sensed it and adapted his original plan. He had split the army, ambushing the western enemy army from all three sides. We knew that would help our cause but the dragon was still approaching. Kenshin front loaded his warriors, and began the long grueling battle with the black dragon. With no monthly cool down spells left, our group would be of little help, so we broke off and went around the backside to take a peak.

The castle was built from shiny black stones that looked like they had been pulled from a riverbed. The walls loomed over us. Guard towers rested upon the castles four corners. We were frozen, mesmerized by its size, leaving ourselves exposed to attack and Hunters were intent on exploiting our mistake. They did little damage from their range but it was still a nuisance. As we rounded the rear, all hope was lost. There was a sole wooden door, reinforced with steel bars, with no chance of infiltrating it. If we could get inside we could kill the caster of the black dragon summon. Once the caster died most summons vanished.

Messages were pouring into our chat board asking for ideas. I had read a book on Genghis Khan recently that made me think of something. It would be risky but it just might work. Our main army was taking heavy losses from the dragon. Our numbers had dwindled down to around fifty. We had no accurate count of how many opponents were left protecting the interior of the castle. I just hoped that their numbers were low enough to make my plan work.

The brush was thick enough to conceal me before I ran at the back door with one of my prized secondary swords. I never used it in PvP because if I died it automatically dropped. Items that dropped upon death became available for anyone that pleased to pick up. It was a rare sword called Colossus. Colossus had the power to destroy barriers, mainly castle doors, by a single user. My sword crashed into the wooden door sending shrapnel flying from the steel bars. Phantom was a couple feet behind me. The only hope we had in entering the castle was that the two hunters on the guard towers were all that was left to protect the rear. Phantom dropped a battering ram and summoned eight simple drones to operate it.

I was slashing wildly at the door with Colossus. The enemy hunters focused fire on Phantom at the start but quickly turned toward me once they saw the sword I was wielding. My life was dropping at a slower rate than I expected until five more DPS users joined in. The door was losing its power and cracks began to split the reinforced wood. Phantom's battering ram was now engulfed in flames from a fire mage. His drones were dropping like flies but he was summoning an army of them, when one died another quickly took its place. I was feeling optimistic at this point because we had the door to half health but then Phantom fell. I didn't see which tower the attacks came from but two players had popped a monthly cool down spell that both struck Phantom in the head. He died quick and I knew I was doomed. The drones perished only seconds later and the battering ram's wheels had collapsed leaving a worthless tipped log smoldering on the ground.

I tried to retreat but another two monthly cool down spells took me from the rear. I gasped as one of my most precious swords dropped to the ground naked and defenseless for anyone to steal. Just before my screen logged off I had seen that our main force had been cut down to a mere twenty-five users, luckily Kenshin was still amongst them. My screen began to flash red, signaling me to leave. I made my way toward the west gate furious, thinking about my lost sword.

The rear gate to the castle creaked open, and a sole vulture of a user came scurrying out to the Colossus sword. His greedy little hands fondled it, admiring the stats before pocketing it in his inventory. He turned and began his cowardice retreat when he stopped dead in his tracks. The door that he had left from seconds ago was now held open in place by tree roots. A sword slammed into his right shoulder from the rear stunning his character for ten seconds, which was all Kira and Knightcr@wler needed to make their grand entrance. Kira cast bubble protection spells that resisted all ranged attacks for a full minute hoping that a warrior wouldn't be waiting on the inside. They lucked out, there was a group of eight approaching from the front gates.

The interior of the castle was barren except for the central castle's keep that usually housed the NPC king. NPC stood for non-player character. There were two ways to win in this PvP game. One was to kill everyone on the opposite team. The other was to take out the castle's king.

Knightcr@wler began sprinting at the warrior and rogues, his hand held fast to his samurai sword resting on his left leg. Kira slammed her staff into the ground creating a thick fog that filled the interior of the castle. The fog would only last for a second before characters switched their vision to see real life but that second was all Knightcr@wler needed. He attacked low at the first warrior spinning his blade upwards, slashing two rogues across the chest. He then did a back flip over his opponents before they had time to switch their visual feed to half and half. They were all still facing Kira when Knightcr@wler did his second attack with a devastating whirlwind slash, sending all eight users flying into the air, keeping them suspended in a tornado.

Kira was now twirling her staff around her body at an incredible speed making it turn bright red and within an instant it was ablaze. She then threw her spinning staff upwards toward the moon and a phoenix rocketed out of its fiery sphere. The phoenix began spitting fireballs as it dove toward helpless groups of users, its wings setting the ground afire in its wake.

The battle was far from over, the black dragon was now heading back to defend the castle. Kira directed her summon toward the castle's keep instructing it to seek and destroy the summoner. The dragon leapt onto the outer wall shrieking with fury as it snapped its monstrous jaws. It sucked in a deep breath, arching its head back as it wiggled its neck. It appeared like he was trying to suck all the stars from the sky to create a night as black as the scales that armored his impenetrable body.

Kira and Knightcr@wler's protection bubble was gone and there was nothing they could do to defend against its deadly fire attack. The dragon then launched his head downward, his mouth wide open with fire dancing and gurgling in his throat. They both crouched down protecting their bodies for what seemed like ages. Nothing came. Kira looked up and the dragon had vanished. Her phoenix! It must have killed the caster. Cheers filled the skies as texts erupted all over their vision. Knightcr@wler was not taking chances though and was already in the process of opening the castle gates. Pure Pwnage users poured into the interior of the castle, taking out the rest of the opposing team. The battle was over and they had come out victorious once again. Equipment and gold was distributed among the clan as the opponents walked to the exit in shame.

Chapter 9: Unordinary Hero
Source: Personal Computer Log
Name: Mr. Smith
Location: VEG Headquarters

Monday mornings plagued my existence. I loathed the cycle of the workweek. It was an institutionalized system that became the punch line of your average Joe. Walking in like zombies, their illusion of disdain almost comical. I could see the eagerness hiding behind their bullshit façade. Their desperate need to tell the grand tales of their superb weekend to their colleagues was pathetic.

Pampered weak social networking parasites from the feel good generation washed over the floor. Dinosaurs like me watched these bits of tar fill our environments, waiting for them to overtake us. This hot thick goo that your body slowly sinks into, the scolding temperature makes you want to scream out, lash out, do anything but be still. I learned the secret was to let it take you like quick sand. I was a lone raptor in a world filled with sheep, a wolf in sheep's clothing.

I liked to stay in my office with the blinds shut on Mondays, to avoid the common courtesies and respects the employees felt obligated to pay. Little children saying hey I was away but now I'm back, like they are checking in from recess. What I wouldn't give for a minute in the interrogation room with any of these sniveling shits.

Today though, I felt more optimistic than most. My plans were falling into place and I left my blinds open to watch the morning ritual. To my surprise, the employees attempted not to indulge in their senseless chatter for the first hour. They didn't like the idea of being under my microscope, but an hour is all they could withstand. Whispers and laughter flooded the blissful silence and a nauseating feeling clenched at the pit of my stomach. I shut the blinds, and after a minute or so the sickness subsided.

Gothamsreckoning was moments away from death and I couldn't let the bottom feeders get to me. I made a phone call to confirm the time, location, and team. The catalyst for Americas rise to its former glory was about to occur. I felt that identical Cliffy death heroin douse my body in pleasure. The finality of it was titillating.

The Chinese will soon grovel at our feet. We will rape their homeland. Yes Rape, say it now. "Rape," I said in a whisper. The word rape never tasted so sweet on my lips. *You will unite the country. You will bring back the spirit of America. The home of the brave will once again be in control. You will bring War, and purify the land...* I felt my mind spinning with excitement and reality went dark.

I came to with an erection digging into my zipper. I wished I were at home for my morning ritual. There was some kind of commotion in the main office.

Terry Hennigan, one of the floor supervisors, was laying into some employee on the floor.

"How long does it take you to do a pole analysis? I gave it to you on Friday morning and I come in to find my desk empty. Could you not find my desk?" Terry yelled.

"I'm sorry sir," is all the man replied. The voice sounded vaguely familiar. I could hear snickering coming from the adjacent cubicles.

"John, I asked you a question. After working here for a year and a half, are you having trouble locating my desk? There has got to be some reason that I don't have the pole, because there is no way that your excuse could be that you didn't have time to finish it. Why don't I show you where my desk is and let me give you a tour of the office while I'm at it? The bathroom is over that way where people produce better shits than the so called work you've been compiling lately," Terry said.

The office erupted in laughter. John hung his head and remained silent. "Here let me show you…" Terry began to pull John's chair out.

"That will be quite alright Terry," I said silencing the room as I walked behind John. "Do you know what the word integrity means?" I said keeping my eyes locked onto Terry so that there was no confusion as to whom I was addressing.

"Sir?" Terry said dumbfounded.

"Integrity Terry, the quality of being honest and having strong moral principles, a quality that I'm afraid you are without," I said in a calm manner.

He fidgeted, "Sir, John had the entire weekend…," he said, the excuse sounding so weak that I could hardly stomach it.

I cut him short saying, "Yes, the whole weekend to do your trivial little exercise. The man apologized did he not?" I said raising my voice now.

"Yes sir," he said.

"Now for the reason," I said interrupting him again. "Every man's got a reason doesn't he?" I looked around the room at all of the tar that filled it, all of the hollow shells of human beings. The decaying wastes that would someday engulf me. "This is the definition of a man with integrity." I placed my hand on John's shoulder. "He is being yelled at for a job that he has an excuse for but he knows that excuses are for the weak and feeble minded. This exquisite employee even apologizes for a crime that he is innocent of as to not shame his superior," I said.

I approached Terry now putting myself between him and John. "I'll tell you why John wasn't doing your weekend project, because of the work he does for me. I personally instructed him to disregard any of your weekend projects so that he may focus on mine. And this employee I'm quite sure can find the bathroom as I'm positive he will be able to find his new office, and position." Terry looked over at his office that I was now eyeing. I walked over to the door and ripped the name Hennigan off of it.

"Please exit the premises, and good luck finding a job after I have John type up a letter to discourage any reputable company from hiring a man like you. I'm sure you'll be delighted by the man's typing skills as well. I've grown quite fond of them myself." Security had already arrived on the scene. Before he could lash out, they had gagged and restrained him.

I enjoyed making sure the employees that left were made an example of. John gave me a subtle bow and walked into his new office without saying a word. He shut the door and closed the blinds. I liked him even more.

Chapter 10: Gotham's Headquarters
Source: Journal
Name: Mark Boggs

A sharp pain shot through my left jaw, head throbbing, my mind numb to the world. I couldn't figure out if I had been hit a minute or three hours ago. My tongue prodded at my cheek barely passing the teeth before I felt the swollen tissue. The acidic taste swirled and turned in my mouth as blood oozed from unknown origins. I swallowed bitterly, the movement of my lips causing a split near my nostrils.

"Who do you work for?" a hard smack across my face shot a rocket filled with adrenaline straight to my brain. My eyes burst open only to be met with a blinding interrogation light. It sent my pupils into shock as they contracted trying to help me cope with the radical change but it was too late. A softball-sized lump of vomit leapt from my esophagus like some sort of alien entity, attacking the chest of my company. It gripped desperately at the cotton woven t-shirt with UNITY written in big block letters on the front.

The shirt depicted the dark silhouette of a man with his fist in the air. His fist was now replaced by my green and yellow abomination. I smiled thinking that it now somewhat resembled the statue of liberty with a green flame. Baring my teeth, I swished the blood through the cracks to taunt my captors, staining my teeth red. A hand lunged at my throat trying to squeeze the life out of me, his grip was soft and I could tell he lacked the training.

I played dumb and let my head go limp, falling to my right hand side, waiting patiently for the man to check my breathing. As I suspected he came in close with his own face only inches from mine. I released all my force driving my head into where I gauged his nose would be but missed by an inch or so.

My rock hard skull crashed hard against his face removing one of his front teeth as he spun backwards colliding into something soft behind him. "Kill that mother fucker!" he screamed as he jumped to his feet. I placed my forehead forward hoping he would be stupid enough to land a blow that would cripple his hand but nothing came. A foot or so before impact he came to an immediate halt. Then I heard nothing, just the trailing footsteps of abandonment.

I was in a warm room and it even felt a bit humid which was strange for this time of winter. Most likely I was underground but I didn't dwell too much on my whereabouts. I focused my attention on my immediate surroundings. Sight was limited to a mere foot in front of me due to the magnitude of the blinding interrogation light. Trying to move my chair seemed futile for it was bolted to the ground. My hands were bound by a series of amateur knots. Given sufficient amount of time, I could untangle them, but I doubted I had long.

They had tied my legs from the thighs to the base of the chair, which rendered the lower half of my body useless. I then tried to move my arms backwards and was relieved to discover that I could almost move them freely. A knot that was meant to bind them tight to my back failed with a little force. I could move them around fifteen inches or so, enough to where I could feel the wall behind me at about thirteen. It felt slick with condensation as if the walls were sweating as much as I was.

A sole set of footsteps began making their way towards me from the distance. I used this time to adjust my eyes to the light to try and give me the highest visibility possible. I was surprised to see a woman enter the room. Whoever pulled the strings had an untrained entourage, which portrayed weakness in my eyes. Although, I had just been caught by their trap.

They had to have some brains in this underground sweat shop. I heard the screech of another chair being pulled away from me, "Who do you work for?" The woman's voice soothed even my painful state.

"Where am I?" I asked while leaning forward, trying to see if I could get a better look at the woman, but no luck. Besides, she was most likely wearing a mask.

"Right now, all you need to know is that you are off the grid." It wasn't a malicious statement and she said it coolly. "What were you doing busting down door 1652?" she asked.

"I work for the police and standard protocol states that we knock down a couple of doors every day until we find someone doing something illegal, didn't you know?" I said. Humor was always my strong suit when it came to the opposite sex, I could sense a smile appearing from somewhere amidst the interrogation light.

"You have no ID card and your prints are unrecognizable. So once again, who do you work for?" She asked.

I thanked the gods that the Green Beret had singed off my fingerprints before I began special ops missions overseas. I never carried identification on me so that hackers couldn't use personal information to try and bypass securities on my account.

I was a ghost, one of the last of my kind, that hadn't been imprinted or tagged with some sort of tracking device.

"The truth is..." I paused and sat motionless looking into the light as if I was contemplating trusting someone.

"What?" She said sweet, breaking the silence.

Her voice was so kind I could barely go on. "The truth is I'm on a secret quest to find eight triangular glowing pieces, that when collected and combined create an artifact called the triforce. I was looking for one of the final pieces and it brought me to apartment 1652. It's the only way for me to free princess Zelda." I leaned in closer as if to whisper. "You have to let me go so I can complete my quest, we are wasting valuable time!" I said.

I felt another smile catch me from across the room. Breathing in deep, I found myself amused. I exhaled through my nostrils, unclogging the dried blood. That's when I first smelt her. It was a burst of spring in the dull winter. The only way I could describe her smell was with a taste, honey whiskey with a mild cigar. She was my heaven. The chair shifted and the smell became distant as she exited.

I sat in a pathetic daze feeling emotions for a scent that I couldn't place with a face. She was a new mental obsession that my body ached for. I snapped myself into focus, moving my arms against the wall, searching for some kind of imperfection.

My hands slid upon the wet wall like a snake slithering this way and that trying to find anything of use. That is when I felt it, a small niche with a bit of something sharp around my elbow. I positioned my fingers so that I could pick at it.

I froze in place hearing someone approach. Small fingers cuddled my face. Sally... she must have followed me here from the ghostel. I was both upset and happy at the same time.

I had trained her from a young age on how to hide and evade detection. She must have been practicing. "Daddy you got yourself all tangled up," she said. "You're so clumsy Papa." I kept calm thinking she might actually believe this was a game I was playing.

"You have very little time to get Daddy free so we can go to ride Ponies tomorrow!!" I said.

At that, Sally unzipped her backpack she always wore, digging deep inside. Her body was halfway in when she found her little red arts and crafts scissors. They were dull but then again the rope wasn't really meant to resist being cut. It was probably the reason why they tied me with so much of it. She began cutting away using the scissors like a saw at one point. Finally, I felt the first bit tear which gave me a lot more movement. She had chosen a good strand to cut because it began unraveling the rest.

I was free in a matter of minutes. I hugged and squeezed her little body as tight as I could. My mind was in perfect focus regardless of the blows to my head. Sally had given me some kind of adrenaline rush knowing that I needed to protect her and keep her safe. They left nothing on me but my watch. They would have taken it if they knew about the button near the top that released a short range EMP burst. It disabled any kind of electronics within a city block. I couldn't really use it to help me escape because my captors most likely carried weapons that would kill me with or without electricity.

I looked around the room for somewhere that I could hide Sally but no luck. I peered through the door, not more than five feet down the hall, a ceiling panel between two light fixtures looked just big enough to fit a child. "We are going to play the hiding game again. I need you to stay as quiet as possible...OK?"

She nodded her head up and down then saluted me with her cute little right hand. "Yes sir," she said in her official sounding voice as she clapped her heels together standing at attention. I pointed to the spot I wanted her to hide and then put a finger to my lips silencing her. I moved swiftly down the hall and hoisted her into the void. She climbed up into the darkness, once safe she peeked back over at me and mimicked the thumbs up that I gave her. It made me rest a little easier having Sally safe, but I was still in a world of trouble.

The building felt like an abandoned FBI headquarters. There were multiple offices and I knew now that I was in fact underground because B5 was posted on a couple of the walls. Sulfur leaks painted the ceilings orange and brown as drips seeped through neglected cracks. Long abandoned I'd have to say. I decided to start picking offices at random, hoping for some luck. Either a solo guard or an ammunitions bunker would be a jackpot but I wasn't feeling optimistic. It reminded me of the game Minesweeper in a way how I would always pick five cells at random hoping for a good outcome but that sixth would always explode when I got greedy. So at the fifth door I decided to proceed with a little more caution. I looked around briefly for some sort of weapon but found only a dull letter opener that I pocketed.

I knew that they would be coming back to interrogate me at some point, and I doubted they would send just one female again that lacked results. The muscle was probably coming next. It was standard procedure to interrogate first with a light bruiser, then someone a little more comfortable and finally where talking failed pain would prevail. I listened to the door hoping for a single set of footsteps but heard nothing, only the constant dripping. I decided to venture on knowing my time was short. There were two sets of staircases. The further set of stairs seemed the most logical option to me.

The stairway only went to L1 so getting out a safe way would be near impossible without running into a guard. I had to scout it though, even if it meant being captured again. A cool breeze hit me as I opened the door, chilled by the fresh winter air. The floor appeared vacant at first but I could hear hushed voices in the distance. I approached the door next to the source and opened it as quiet as possible, slipping inside with my letter opener gripped in my right hand. To my surprise there was a door inside the room leading into the adjacent office where the voices were. I got up close to it, so close that their voices were almost decipherable. It was five men and one woman. I pressed my ear firm to wood and listened. "He won't talk, and it will take a couple of hours to hack his Jackers." The soft female voice said.

"He couldn't be a cop, he would have had backup and the police would be on us by now," said a man positioned against the far wall.

"He had to have been looking for Gothamsreckoning. He could be a friendly." This voice made the door vibrate, he was right next to me resting with some body part flush against the thin layer of wood.

"Let's just beat it out of him, we can't risk him capturing you." My ears perked up and my heartbeat increased as adrenaline rushed through my veins. Gothamsreckoning was just beyond this one-inch wooden barrier.

I rose up slow as to not alert, and then gauged the power of my kick. I lunged forward feeling the force hit hard against the shoulder and head of the unknown body resting on the other side. The room had little time to react as I slid in like lightning grabbing the woman roughly around the chest, my letter opener pressed firm to her throat. Four guns were drawn and aiming in my direction as I backed us against the closest corner.

Her hair was intoxicating, dark curly Caribbean hair complementing her honey beige skin, tossed across my steady hand as I inched her further into a defensive position. One man lay stunned on the ground trying to regain total consciousness. His arms and legs wobbled as he braced himself against a desk to gain composure. "How did you find me?" A girl said in a voice that sounded eerily familiar. I had only briefly heard it after her screams.

There she was, the helpless little girl with my rough bandaging tarnishing her innocent face just below her eye. She had healed well in just a day. She was sitting with her knees together, crouched in a little nook between two desks on the far wall. My grip loosened for a split second but I refocused. "You don't need to save me from these people. They are friends." She said as if I was her protector. This changed everything, my mind jumped to multiple outcomes of how this would play out.

"Bell, how... how do you know this man?" the guy asked from the corner of the room, his desert eagle still trying to get a fix on my forehead. Bell looked around and lowered her head in shame.

"Bell, speak now!" The woman in my grasps said, fighting the words against my blade pressed firmly to her esophagus.

"I was going to tell you but I didn't want you to worry. I was attacked on my way home last night... nothing happened though because of my hero. He saved me. How did you find me my knight?"

The girl was of a different breed and had obviously been told way too many fairy tales. Before I could answer, I heard it, the soft click of a Rabid X-52. Rabid X-52's were standard issue to special ops police forces. They were automatic assault rifles with five different types of ammunition. Near the base of the rifle lay five cartridge barrels that held around fifty rounds. Armor piercing rounds were the ammo of choice for entrance with lethal purpose. Gas rounds were preferred in low ventilated rooms, each one releasing a concentrated volume of H2S gas. Odorless and lethal, you were dead in seconds. Taser rounds were short ranged but a pain in the ass. They would not only kill but they released a coil of thin metal wire connected to the base of the barrel. Each one was electrically charged and when sprayed across a room it was like a spider setting a web that made it impossible to escape from. The fourth type was an explosive round, but the fifth were my favorite. The fifth type of round was a proximity mine. Each bullet was tipped with four metal barbs that extended from the head and looked like eagle claws upon release. They would penetrate whatever surface you shot them at and then arm. Any kind of motion would activate them, causing a lethal focused explosion. Escaping the police by backtracking wasn't an option.

That soft click was the sound that only a Rabid X-52 made when engaging the ammunition of choice. It was too late to alarm them all, some would die, but I doubted they were in a position to take the building yet. I searched the hips of the woman finding my Glock pressed against her side. The gun jumped into my hand like an old friend, my pointer finger stroking its trigger. I felt a cool calmness wash over me before the storm, and then I shouted, "BELL, BELLY DOWN NOW, EVERYONE BEHIND ME." I twirled around throwing my captive diving toward the door as armor piercing rounds broke through the window taking one of the men in the back of the skull and the other two through the chest. The man standing near the desk took one to the left shoulder sending him screaming to the floor. Only one of the gang made it down unscathed. I opened the door, dragging the woman outside, as Bell crawled quickly after. It only took another couple of seconds for them to breach the windows and then they were in.

I was in luck, because they hadn't come through any other entrance yet. They had to attack prematurely due to my actions. I was not about to let some rookie shit get the best of me. Police were almost impossible to escape, due to their multitude of tracking devices. Every Police helmet came equipped with a streaming video camera that was monitored by a hive of brains. Once your face was identified you were toast. Luckily I had tools to help me survive a little bit longer and I intended on using them. I jumped up, grabbing Bell by the hand and began sprinting toward the stairwell while I pushed the EMP burst on my watch.

During a raid police were very susceptible to this attack because they relied on all of their communications being linked to give the maximum percentage of success. EMP bursts were not available to citizens and the makeshift ones created on the streets were all too weak to shut down even the camera links on their helmets. Mine was acquired through my prior profession. I knew that the burst would buy us some time, but only a minute or two. Eventually the orders would be given to the worker ants by some form of communication to seek and destroy.

One of the gung ho warriors wasn't waiting for his god to answer and he rounded the corner shooting two or three explosive rounds into the chest and abdomen of the unscathed man trailing twenty or so steps behind us. His body exploded before he could register the pain. It was a terrible thing to do to a man but I imagine this cowboy hadn't gotten to fire his gun on a live mission. Most cops were pumped so full of video game adrenaline and simulated battle that the kill they had just made wouldn't register until much later. Right now he was trigger happy and years from now he would be on a couch in some simulated psychiatrists office talking about the deep seeded issues that all derived from this very moment.

I rounded the corner and busted through the stair doors. "Quickly, is there any secondary route for escape?" The woman looked at me stunned as I stopped on B2. Blood covered her face and she looked half in shock. I grabbed her by the arms and shook her wildly. "This isn't a fucking game or one of your stupid VEG simulations. You must have some sort of fail-safe route in this place. These cops were sent to kill not wound."

She blinked and started slowly, "A... a crawl space. Yes a crawl space on B5 through one of the offices, it leads four blocks from here." Focus came into her eyes. More importantly a wave of emotion flew over me knowing I could easily grab Sally on the way down. We continued down to the depths of the facility.

"I've got to grab my daughter," I yelled as we approached the door to B5.

"Your daughter?" The woman still sounded a little stunned.

"Yes she came and rescued me, it will only take a second."

I ran to Sally's hiding place and whistled the ok signal, which I had taught her at a young age. I had two whistles, turn and run and all ok. She enjoyed doing them and I made up a short story that comforted her about how mother and father birds do this in the wild to warn each other of predators. Her little head poked out of the black abyss in the ceiling and she smiled, jumping into my arms. The woman and little girl looked at us bewildered. I grabbed Sally's hand and said "this is my daughter, I need to get us out of here." The woman still looked to be in complete shock, her eyes bouncing between Sally and I.

"Follow me" she finally forced out. We ended up in the same office I had searched earlier for a weapon. She pushed a filing cabinet out of the way to reveal a small concrete crawl space to safety.

Chapter 11: Digital Love
Time: Six Years Prior
Source: Personal Computer Log
User: Evo

Standing outside the gates, minutes rolled by like hours, hoping that my plan had been successful. I was fidgeting, a habit I did when I was furious, because I had to lose my Colossus blade to bait the enemy into opening their gate.

Phantom was sitting on a bench next to me rocking slowly back and forth. There was no way they would be stupid enough to fall for such a simple trick. I began pacing back and forth starring at the ground when two arms wrapped around my sides lifting me in the air.

"You dog you!" Knightcr@wler howled as he hugged me. "The noobs fell for it!"

"What!?" I said, with excitement filling my chest.

"I mean truly, it only worked because Kira and I are such pros. A noob like you and Phantom would have never been able to pull it off inside." Phantom jumped up tackling Knightcr@wler at the waist. They both began wrestling on the concrete.

"And Kira?" I asked.

"Alive, and out of spells for the next year," Kira said slipping in to give me a warm hug. She had a cute little smile on her face when she released me.

"What is it?" I asked.

"Men just don't know when to put away their swords," She said with a devilish smile as she pulled out my Colossus sword from her inventory. A rush of emotion over took me and before I could stop myself I had my arms wrapped around Kira, bear hugging her.

"Oh make out already," Phantom said breaking up our moment.

I released her and jumped at Phantom, the three of us now wrestling on the concrete. "Should I lend an extra rod for your hot threesome?" Kira asked. We all laughed and stood up brushing the dust from our clothes.

"Would any of you fine gentleman do me the honor of escorting me home tonight? I hear there are some disgruntled VEG players that just lost a match, and might be exacting revenge against those responsible for their loss," Kira said smiling, pleased with her own sarcasm.

Phantom and Knightcr@wler both said at once, "Evo can do it." Phantom immediately punched Knightcr@wler in the arm, both of them giggling like immature little girls.

"Evo, you free?" Kira said in a nonchalant manner.

"Sure," I said. "I completely agree, having two noobs walk you home wouldn't be safe," I added, taunting them both. "Please, the only one that's noob at anything is you at getting women. We gotta throw you a bone once in a while. No offense Kira," said Phantom. I gave him a quick glare.

"None taken, but remember Phantom it's not pro if you pay for it," Kira said smiling as she turned and began to walk away, not waiting for Phantom's smart-ass rebuttal. I quickly followed but not before throwing them both a smile and my middle finger. "Noob" was a term gamers used for someone that was new to anything and therefore unskilled. It was one of our favorite insults.

The walk home was short but lasted an eternity in my mind. My right arm felt heavy, hanging sluggish at my side in an awkward fashion. I knew I wanted to hold her hand but I, being the furthest from suave and smooth, had no inkling of how to do so. Especially with her arms crossed, warming her body against the cold of the early morning hours. *A girl like Kira could never like a guy like me; she's hit on by everyone in our clan and had most likely heard it all. You're an idiot, you think just because she smiles at you that she wants something to do with you. She smiles and jokes with everyone. What makes you so special? But... if there is something there, this is your only chance to find out. You'll never get an opportunity like this again. Just do something... test the waters* - I thought moving a little bit closer to her.

I began swinging my awkward arm a little bit more directly to graze the side of her voluptuous hips. She made no reaction to the first graze. My penis on the other hand began protruding from the front of my pants and I now had another problem that I hoped she didn't notice. *Jesus one little graze and you're already rearing to go. She's going to think you are a pervert, a premature overly aggressive ape that can't keep it in his pants. Not to mention you haven't said a word to her in the last...well I don't know how long....*

Her arms unfolded and dropped to her side, breaking my thoughts. I swung my arm once more in her direction and this time it grazed the back of her soft hand. Our hands danced around each others. They touched lightly until they swung in unison, slowly losing motion until I went for it, grabbing her entire hand. Her fingers squeezed mine as I slid my thumb around the back of her pinky and ring finger.

This felt almost like a strategy game and I was finally gaining a little control. My confidence level was beginning to rise almost as much as my penis had. I began to think of those Japanese dating games where you had to get enough money to buy the girl gifts to make her like you enough to get to the point where she would invite you back to her place. Then you would have to use cheesy lines to get her interested enough to kiss you. If you got the kiss you spent more money and time to get her into bed. It took ages to get her clothes off and any false move decreased all the favor points you had worked so hard for. The funny thing was that I spent hours on those games just to get a virtual girl's clothes off so she would sleep with me. At that very moment I realized how sad and pathetic I was.

Kira came to a stop and she pulled on my arm to make me halt, probably seeing that I was in lala land. "This is me," she said, looking up at a four story brick built apartment building. "That was some match today."

"Yeah," I said laughing a little bit like a goof. "Thank you, for retrieving my sword, you have no idea how much that meant to me."

"Yeah well, you would have done the same for me, besides it was your idea that won us the match," she said, followed by an awkward silence.

I turned to face her, and her eyes shied away from me a bit. Something strong came over me at that very moment and I cupped her cheek, turning her face back up toward me, "come here." My face went in close and she responded beautifully, her lips blossoming out toward my own until they met.

I kissed her long and hard, sliding my right hand down the small of her back. Our tongues played around with each other teasing and tickling. She pressed the entirety of her body up against mine, the warmth of her core erupting my sexual urges. Pulling away she looked up at me and asked the one thing that every man dies to hear, "You want to come up?"

When we arrived at her place, I felt like the woman for the first time. She pulled me into her bedroom like a savage, throwing me down hard upon her bed, placing my Jackers on my head. Turning on her heels, she bumped me with her bottom sending me backwards onto my elbows. Her hips swayed back and forth like a little temptress as she walked toward her closet.

The room was spacious with modern décor. Japanese floral portraits of cherry blossoms in bloom hung on two of the walls with dim lights illuminating them from behind, casting beautiful shadows on the floor. A one-foot wide French drain lined the perimeter of her bed filled with smooth black and white riverbed stones. I took my shoes off, resting my bare feet upon them, digging my toes into the voids between.

Trance music poured into the room with subtle hints of jazz. She came out of the bathroom wearing nothing but her VEG gear. Of course through my Jackers she was covered in beautiful spandex like lingerie that hugged her seductive form. She reminded me of Mystique from X-Men. Her hips danced back and forth with the rhythm of the music as she began to feel herself, her hands sliding up her sides and into the air. To my astonishment, the spots she touched, her augmented lingerie disappeared. She then rubbed over the topside of her breasts throwing her head back, her hair swooping behind her. I stood up without even realizing it, entranced by her dancing. The intensity of the song began to increase and now she was waving her unexposed breasts back and forth in front of me. Finally she slid her hands over the front of each of them tickling her own erect nipples as they passed.

Her body was that of a goddess. She approached me with her head tilted down to the degree that she looked like a predator with her eyes set on her prey. Lunging at me like a lion, she pressed her body firmly against mine. Her hands squeezing my butt while she kissed me. One of her hands slid down the front of my pants, her thumb tickling my belly button as it passed, until she reached the bulge of my penis. "Now let's see how you use this rod," she said while flashing that devilish smile she always used.

It felt like a minute later but the memory would bury itself somewhere in my mind for a lifetime. She was everything I'd imagined she would be and more. We tangled our naked bodies together in a warm cocoon on top of her sweat stained white sheets and fell asleep. It was a perfect end to a perfect day.

After a maze of concrete tunnels, we exited into a storage garage. There was a single car parked inside and I was ecstatic when I saw the old modified Mustang muscle car. "Runs on diesel?" I asked as she searched through a wall unit for the keys. "Of course," she said, manually unlocking the doors. She was smart. Ninety nine percent of the cars on the street were electric. It was too expensive to afford a gas or diesel run car and they had been outlawed several years ago. Still they blended in due to the fact that electric cars were now manufactured to mimic the feel of these dinosaurs. The police always caught anyone they were in pursuit of because each of their cars came equipped with a focused EMP burst that shut down your engine and rendered your car useless. Sally and I took the back seat and the woman and Bell climbed in front. The garage door hissed open and we were off into the early morning sunrise.

We drove for a good hour, driving into hill country that I didn't know existed. We came to a stop at a secluded cabin that lay on a hilltop. It was the first time I had been in a non-automated house in a while. All the walls were made from timber and the house was plain and quaint on the inside.

The ladies went and washed up upon arrival while I stocked the fireplace. An hour later we were all resting silently around the warmth of the crackling fire. The woman and Bell looked at Sally and I with strange glances. "How...how old is your daughter?" She broke the silence with a question.

"She just turned ten a week ago."

Sally pulled on my sleeve. "The picture daddy, show them the picture."

I pulled a wrinkled picture from my wallet and showed it to the woman and Bell. It was a picture of her on her fifth birthday with a ribbon in her hair standing next to a little white pony. She was all smiles and I smiled a little bit thinking of the day.

"She's beautiful," the woman said. She then grabbed Bell and squeezed her tightly as if it just registered that they were alive and safe. Then she began to weep letting out short sobs. "He was the only chance we had," she said, with her head buried in her arms.

"Who?" I knew before she even answered.

"GOTHAMS RECKONING."

There goes my payday. "Who was he?"

"Someone who could have saved us all" she whispered.

The sunlight gripped my eyelids ripping them open from their sleep state. I tried to focus but the room blurred and twisted. It had been ages since I slept and I couldn't remember how I got into bed. Red goo coated the roof of my mouth and it felt sticky as I slid my tongue along it. The cheap merlot came crashing back into my memory as well as the prior day's events. I was out of a job and most likely a fugitive on the run with a useless woman and her daughter.

Sally was still sleeping on the bed curled up next to me. I could hear the front door whisper open and soft footsteps treading somewhere in the living room, or at least where I thought I remembered the living room was. I pulled out my pistol and slipped out of bed. It was too easy to become comfortable in a homey environment such as this. A surreal log cabin with comfy beds in the middle of nowhere felt like a vacation I had dreamt up during my drunken stupor.

I slid out of the door silently, hoping that the wooden flooring wouldn't deceive my steps. A man around six foot two inches was walking past the living room and down an adjacent hallway. I slipped in behind him tracing his footsteps. He heard me at the last second but it was too late. I had my Glock 17 pressed coldly to the back of his head. "Hello friend," I said.

He was a little bit larger than I expected but his posture was sluggish. "Please, p-please don't hu... hurt me. I'm a f-friend," he stuttered. The man sounded younger than I expected. I loosened my grip on the pistol. He rounded in an instant grabbing my gun, twisting it out of my hand, his shoulders and posture now that of a trained warrior. I was off my feet before I could make a noise and he had my Glock 17 pointed directly between my eyes. "Hello friend indeed," he said boasting. For a second his gun waivered and his eyes flashed some kind of concern or recognition but only for a second and then he focused again. "Silvia!" he yelled out. Footsteps came running from another hallway and came to a dead stop behind me.

"He's ok, he's with us Evo," Silvia said.

Silvia... it sounded sweet on the tongue. I had never even taken the time to ask for her name. She had saved my life and most importantly my daughter.

"What the hell is he doing here?" Evo said.

"He saved us from the cops in our city bunker" she said as she pulled the gun down.

He raised it back up defiantly. "Did it ever occur to you that he was the one that called the cops?" he said.

"He wouldn't have done that, he almost lost his life in the process. We can trust him," Silvia said.

"That is exactly what the police would want you to think. You know more than anyone that this is the way they infiltrate a tight knit group. They make you think that he was there to save you. For Christ's sake he could be wearing a wire right now. Check him," he said motioning the gun at my chest.

I decided this debate had gone on long enough. "I'll check myself." I said ripping open my shirt to show my bare chest painted with old war scars. Silvia gasped and Evo lowered the gun a bit. "Listen Evo, whatever kind of name that is. I'm a collections agent and I was tracking Gothamsreckoning when I bumped into your girlfriend here. I work alone or else I don't get paid and now that Gothamsreckoning is dead and I helped aid some of his crew in escaping, I'm in the same boat as you." I said standing up pushing the gun aside.

Evo looked hard at Silvia and then turned back toward me. "A fucking collections agent. Great man to have on our side. He would have taken us all to prison for fucking money if given the chance," he said waving his gun.

"Who said 'would have?' I'm rather fond of the idea of taking you in right now, but I doubt you'd be worth much." I said taunting him. I saw the butt end of the pistol coming as the final word came out of my mouth and I had him just where I wanted him. I slid right and drove my knee straight up into his chest catching the pistol in the air as I reversed his grip and twisted his arm behind his back. A kick to the back sent him crashing into a picture frame, which fell and shattered on the ground. I noticed the painting in the broken frame was of two wolves in the heat of battle over a dead carcass on the ground and it made me smile a bit.

"You mother fucker." He rose to his feet and charged.

"QUIT IT!" Bell screamed stopping him dead in his tracks. The little girl was quiet when she wanted to be, I didn't even hear her approach.

"We'll finish this later," Evo said before turning and storming out of the cabin.

Silvia had a puzzled look on her face. "You wouldn't take us in would you?" she asked, her pupils dilated making them appear as innocent as a kittens.

I put my hand on her shoulder and rubbed it down her arm, "Not after what you did for me and my daughter." I suddenly felt like it was an awkward thing to do and removed my hand coldly. I don't know why I attempted to comfort her but she smiled at me and made it all worth it. That is when I realized that this woman would be the death of me.

Chapter 13: Summer
Time: Five Years Prior
Source: Personal Computer log
User: Evo

Last year was the budding of Kira and I's relationship. Phantom and Knightcr@wler took the news of us dating well, only fussing when it interfered with our quests and guild raids. They were like our two children that we constantly had to appease. We were all sitting in Phantom's basement, a hideout so to speak, on the brim of summer.

The room bore a masquerade of retro gaming collages. Nintendo Power posters were strewn about, honoring the roots of grinding it out. Grinders was a term loosely given to gamers that spent countless hours doing repetitive game play with the intent of having an extra advantage in the quests to come. The first grinders were that of old RPG games like Final Fantasy that sat in lower level based zones, spending days leveling up so that when they continued they had the advantage. Those players were the bread and butter of VEG users. Patience was one of the strongest virtues we had in our clan.

I was connected to this group because they were true gamers. Guys like us respected the origins of the movement. There was a huge cult following of console games, being the roots and or catalyst for VEG's creation. Knowing those games and original works, now considered art, helped in questing. Most VEG users studied everything about the generation that Charles Sanders lived in because of how much help it gave in questing. He left secrets and Easter eggs for the dedicated fans. It was what most of us lived for, solving the riddles that no one else could. The more you knew about the history of games the better equipped you were for VEG.

Phantom and Knightcr@wler were sitting Indian style in front of a screen that covered the whole basement wall, playing excite bike on the original Nintendo. Excite Bike was a motocross racing video game that they had spent months on the very first level. They went back and forth racing single player, trying to break each other's fastest time. Any slight mistake made the difference between failure and a perfect run. It didn't help that when either one of them raced they took it upon themselves to talk as much trash as possible during the minutes of game play.

"So what's the plan for this summer guys?" I said after Phantom's race finished without breaking the record.

"You mean other than you and Kira's marriage and your constant attempts at making ugly abomination babies? Kira, you have thought about how your children will turn out right?" Phantom asked, still sticking it to the both of us every chance he got. Knightcr@wler smiled snatching the controller from Phantom's hands.

"Yes, other than that. I mostly was referring to VEG," I said, knowing that the best method to overt Phantom's wrath was to accept his banter with a smile. Phantom was too quick witted for anyone to match his shit talking. The only one that even came close with clever quips was Kira.

"I say we do the same thing we do every summer," Knightcr@wler said and at once Phantom and Kira both chimed in, "TRY AND TAKE OVER THE WORLD!" They loved getting the chance to reference the television show Pinky and the Brain. We had finished gathering the best equipment from PvP since we currently held the number one spot in the United States, so like always, we had the entire summer free to do what we wanted.

"Ender's Quest," Knightcr@wler said in a soft whisper.

"My GOD, every single summer... what is it with you and this mythical quest?" Phantom scolded Knightcr@wler jarring the controller from his hand mid turn after a single crash. "It doesn't exist! It's a stupid fucking blogger that got his kicks off sending Easter Bunny believers like yourself on his trail of shit. Besides, if Charles Sanders did invent the greatest hidden quest, wouldn't you think that someone would have found it by now? I mean did you read the description of the item that blogging loon thinks is at the end of his rabbit hole? It's a sword that literally makes you invulnerable and honestly how would he even know?" Phantom threw the controller after his bike overheated. It shattered against the wall, his player in the game cooled off on the side of the 8-bit track.

Phantom rose calmly and printed another controller from Knightcr@wler's 3D printer. 3D printers were capable of building anything at this point and were standard in every household across America. Knightcr@wler had an extension on his house that was printed by one, as did most of the houses in his neighborhood.

Knightcr@wler looked annoyed waiting for the controller to finish, "Alright, what do we know? We know that Charles Sanders favorite book was Ender's Game. He said that Ender was the only character that he had a true connection with. In a number of his first augmented quests he had elements from each of the Ender's series books." With a flick of Knightcr@wler's finger, virtual screens appeared, suspended in midair showing playbacks of multiple quests that had Ender's Game elements.

"The key though, is that Charles loved Ender, related with him and understood the battles and trials he endured to become a leader. One of the main obstacles in Ender's youth is the free roam adventure game that focused on his psyche. It made him face his deep-seeded fears and manifested negative character attributes. I think that game struck a chord with Charles, the parallels with his life were uncanny."

All of the virtual screens changed abruptly, and were now showing Ender morphing into a rat and running up to a Giant with two different potions. "I've always thought that there was a version of the free roam Giant's Drink game somewhere in VEG. I hadn't found it because I was looking in the wrong place." Knightcr@wler had all the screens showing the countless quests and journeys we as a group had gone on in prior summers. "So if you were Charles Sanders where would you hide the first clue of an undetectable quest?" Knightcr@wler looked around at us with an excitement in his eyes that I hadn't thought possible.

"Probably somewhere that no one in the world would be clever enough to think of except for... Oh my god Knightcr@wler!" Phantom said pretending to be bored with the conversation.

Knightcr@wler ignored him and continued with even more excitement. "In the real world!!" he paused again waiting for our reaction. "Look, Charles was a huge fan of adventure, right? You know Indiana Jones, The Goonies and all of the classics. A man that spent his early years before video games would want our generation to unplug and realize that VEG isn't everything. It was right there in front of me all along but I couldn't detach myself from the never-ending amounts of code to search. The real kicker was

Ender's Universe in VEG. It had everyone looking in the wrong place. A user could spend a lifetime searching its vastness. When you overload a system with arenas and maps it sends people down a rabbit hole that will never end, but if we search in the real world first we might find the beginning. I've been searching every summer and I think I finally found something," Knightcr@wler said.

Kira actually moved forward a little bit taking remote interest and to my surprise Phantom dropped the newly finished controller mid game and turned around. "Where?" Phantom asked.

"No forget it, it's stupid... Let's just do something else this summer." Knightcr@wler picked up the controller like he hadn't just hooked us and was now toying with Phantom.

"You little," Phantom said, attacking Knightcr@wler. They both rolled around on the floor wrestling for a bit with spurts of laughter and banter.

"Alright, alright," Knightcr@wler said sitting upright. "Put on your Jacks."

"Jacks" was the term Knightcr@wler used for the VEG's Jackers, and he was hoping that the lingo would catch on. It was used amongst our clan, but it hadn't fully hit amongst the other users of the world. He placed a virtual screen in front of us and began again. "Alright, so going back to the whole Giant's drink quest. An unknown billionaire purchased a good amount of land in a small town in Utah. Three lots to be precise, and each purchased under someone else's name as to not reveal his own identity."

The excitement started to rise in Knightcr@wler's voice. "On these plots of land the man built three establishments.

The first was an Inn that was made in the shape of an egg called Weird Egg Inn, one of those wannabe strange destinations in the US for road trippers. On the second plot, an arcade was built called Gamer Needs that paid homage to the old cartridge systems as well as pinball machines, and the best arcade games over the last century. On the final plot of land, the unknown investor built a bar called Dethroned the Wolf. It was the only one of the establishments that saw any profit, even with its obscure name. The interesting part of these investments is that the bar started construction three years before the Inn and the arcade yet it finished two years after the other two completed. Another curious part about the bar's construction is that it was the only one of the three that was blocked from public view by a fifty-foot concrete wall. The entire plot of land extends a good football field distance behind the establishment."

Phantom interrupted Knightcr@wler, "so what does any of it have to do with Charles Sanders or Enders Quest?"

Knightcr@wler disregarded his outburst and continued in a calm manner. "Weird Egg Inn, Gamer Needs, and Dethroned the Wolf are all curious names don't you think?" He looked around at us, nodding as if we understood where he was going with all of this. "They are all anagrams!" he said with a smile plastered across his face.

"What?" Kira said.

"Anagrams! Letters rearranged to create a new word or phrase. It was Charles Sanders favorite type of word play," Knightcr@wler said and without waiting for us to take it in he began writing the three establishment's names up in virtual space.

"Look, Weird Egg Inn." He wrote the glowing letters in the air and then moved them around with his hands to form two words. I read it slowly, "Ender... Wiggin." "YES!" he said now jumping to his feet. "Gamer Needs, becomes Ender's Game and finally the one that brings us back to my first idea is Dethroned the Wolf!"

He rearranged the letters slowly as we all watched mesmerized and there it was clear as day "The End Of The World,"

Phantom whispered. His eyes were locked upon the letters. "Exactly!" Knightcr@wler was becoming more and more exuberant.

"In the first book Ender's Game, after Ender kills the giant, drowns the wolves, and lowers himself down into the well, he comes across a door that has THE END OF THE WORLD written in glowing emeralds on it. The bar is the key. Why would a nine hundred square foot building take eight years to complete? Charles must have built an underground adventure and we all have to travel to Utah to check it out!"

"Slow down there old Indiana. You want us all to fly across the country to spend part of our summer in exotic Utah, so we can break into a bar that could potentially have an underground fortress that leads us to the mythical best item in VEG?" Phantom said.

"Yes," was all Knightcr@wler could manage.

"Sounds good, I'm in... but me and you are going to make babies in that Weird Egg Inn while Evo and Kira watch," Phantom said as he grabbed Knightcr@wler's hand and brought him in for a hug.

"Quit it, you know your guys' homoerotic fantasies turn me on," Kira said as she came in closer to the two.

"There is a good chance we will all come back Mormons but I'm in," I said smiling. I joined the group in the center of the room and felt whole.

I had spent so many years as an outcast to society that it now almost hurt to feel so accepted and loved. I looked around at my three best friends and thought I couldn't picture a better life for myself. Still something felt surreal as if it could be taken from me in a flash. Like an illusory world was about to disappear, leaving only that lonely feeling that used to fill me. Nights spent sitting in front of a computer screen alone, telling myself that my online friends were all I needed. You wanted to leave but as the real world relationships fell apart around you, new cyber relationships replaced them. The feeling was fresh now, bathing my body in the old senses. I wanted to leave it but I might miss something, fall behind and become unwanted in the game world. Miss something was all I was doing. I was missing the marrow of life, the companionship of others, and the physical and mental interaction that makes us human. VEG changed that, now I had a family that cared for me and was there for me. I was... happy.

Chapter 14: New Friends, New Enemies
Source: Journal
Name: Mark Boggs

Silvia and Evo had spent most of the morning walking together. The man was aggressive and gave me an unsettling feeling. Silvia tried to make amends between us but I didn't trust him. There was something he was hiding, something behind those eyes. They recognized me, but how. Nothing in my memory could recall his face, I reached back deep only to be met with a throbbing headache. She assured me of his credibility before their little stroll. Some VEG wiz that was top of the scoreboard five years ago but stopped the game cold turkey for some unknown reason. That was when Gothamsreckoning scooped him up for his so-called master plan. Dead men's plans rarely seem to work out. Regardless they wouldn't let me join their little morning hike so I stayed in.

I sat inside playing with Bell and Sally. Bell had pulled out a Briar Rabbit tea set that we were currently sitting around. I had to help her boil the water but once the tea was in the pot she took over, pouring each of our tiny cups in turn. I watched her overload them with cream, which made the once clear tea turn murky like muddy water.

She played the host well, asking us each if we would like one or two cubes of sugar. She helped herself to four and because I wasn't her parent I didn't object but I knew that in the next hour she was going to be charged like the Energizer Bunny. Sally wanted one but Bell gave her two anyways saying "girls are sweet so we need more sugar to keep us that way." She then began directing the gossip. "My mother tells me that the government is going to cause an enormous war with the way they are using VEG."

I decided to take it upon myself to get some more information out of this comical child. "Well what does your father say?"

Bell flinched a little and I felt bad for asking the question but she reacted like a lady. She placed her teacup on its baby saucer and dabbed her lips with her napkin. "My father would agree."

I decided to drop the question knowing from her reaction that he wasn't in the picture. "Who would we go to war with?" I asked.

"Well the Chinese of course," she let out a laugh from what I imagine she thought an older sophisticated lady would sound like.

"Well then how will we prevent this Chinese American war?" I asked playing into her questioning.

"Us," Silvia said as she walked through the door with Evo. Evo browsed the room, his face focused on our tea party and then he walked out of the cabin.

"Mr. Evo doesn't look like he will be joining us for a spot of tea Bell." I said with my best British accent. Bell giggled and took a sip of her tea dancing her head back and forth to some imaginary music.

"Mark, we have some business to discuss," Silvia said with a serious look on her face.

"May I be excused madam?" I said remembering my courtesies.

"Yes, yes, leave us ladies so we can gossip while you're gone," Bell said. I placed my teacup down in a dainty fashion and got up to walk outside with Silvia.

Outside Silvia didn't spare any time, "We need to take a trip into the city. Due to unforeseen circumstances we have been forced to act quicker than we anticipated. I have very little time to fill you in on what's going on. What do you know about the government's plan for VEG?"

I was taken aback by how forward she was being. "Other than the fact that they want to revolutionize the world?" I said in a sarcastic manner.

"Charles Sanders wanted to revolutionize the world. The government, we figured just wanted to make a profit but after the blackout we know they are up to more than that."

"The blackout?" I questioned.

"My god do you watch the news or read the papers?" she said. I shrugged. "Yes, the blackout. Just last week China became a dead zone, and the government has conveniently placed the blame on a group of hackers led by the notorious Gothamsreckoning. Once China's economy drops below America's there will be an all-out witch-hunt for Gothamsreckoning. With all of us dead, the government can keep hunting a ghost forever and China will have no footing with the rest of the world on scaling an attack. The fact that we are alive is a huge inconvenience to them because if word got out that we weren't responsible for the attack, China would have more than enough reasons to go to war," she said. Her eyes were steady and true. I had done enough human lie detecting over the years to know that she truly believed what she was telling me.

"I doubt the entire government is against China," I said playing the devil's advocate. We learned with conspiracy theorists that it is best to question them at least once.

"Well not the entire government of course but an agency within the government," she said visibly frustrated with my answer.

"If Gothamsreckoning doesn't want to make China a blackout zone and cause a global war as you say, then what does he want to do?" I asked still not seeing what their role in this whole situation was.

"Our plan is to take control of VEG and make America a dead zone as well, for the time being. China is already skeptical about the blackout and combined with the fact that VEG users are physically fit enough to be super soldiers, it appears as though America is preparing for war. If we black out America as well, it will put those conspiracies to rest, giving us time to repair our relationship with them before bringing it back online. VEG will revolutionize the world one day, but for now, that utopia will have to wait," she said.

"How does your group plan to take control of VEG? You better have one hell of a programmer and an army of hackers," I said realizing the fault in my last statement right after it leapt from my lips. Of course Gothamsreckoning had an army of hackers, it was the sole reason I was hunting the user and his army in the first place.

"We plan to infiltrate the VEG headquarters within New York City and install a virus designed to destroy source code in the system," she said.

"Listen I'm no guru with the whole VEG system but I know that the system administrators aren't pushovers. They are most likely as skilled as you and your little gang, not to mention the fact that the VEG headquarters will be guarded to the teeth," I said.

"That's true which is why timing is everything. Once a year the government programming squad has a PVP match open to any and all VEG players. They have unlimited resources and have bought almost every precious artifact and summon in the game. They will be near impossible to beat, which is why we have been building an army of the greatest VEGERs. Charles Sanders's last gift before departing VEG was that if you lost in a PVP arena then you would be locked out of VEG, regardless of status. We will challenge the government's tech team, beat them, and on the same night take down the entire system. There will probably be a small group of source code slaves left but with a little force they should fold with the rest of their army gone," she said.

I felt a purpose for the first time in a while. I hated VEG players with a passion so I was fully onboard for a takedown of the entire system. We had a plan, a rough and gutsy plan, but it was something. "My daughter and I are with you," I said. She hugged me long and hard and I felt myself squeezing her back. It was the first physical connection that I had made with a woman in a long time or ever.

"I trust you Mark. I trust you more than I should after this short amount of a time. Which is why I'm going to trust you even more now." She leaned in close to my ear. I could feel her soft breath upon it. "I am Gothamsreckoning."

The room was metallic, an underground fallout shelter that resembled the one in the Cheyenne mountains. The pinnacle of our technology during the fifties sat in an eternal slumber, now covered in several inches of dust. All my forgotten old friends beeped the tune of a dying soul on the final moments of life support. There would be no savior for them, as there was no savior for me.

Vultures starred at me, perched in their comfy nests of seats, reviewing paperwork as a formality. They eyed me like a carcass, awaiting my final death spasms so that they could devour my rotting flesh.

Gothamsreckoning had escaped my foolproof plan. These ancients relied on me to get the job done. Observers, is what I liked to call them, too weak to carry out the dirty work themselves. They weren't men, they weren't even human. They spoke in a vague new dialect that was open to interpretation. It was developed for the sole purpose of deniability; nothing said could incriminate them. Over time, dinosaurs like me learned to decipher it.

The language went as follows: *General Davis has become a problem* – Kill Davis, leave no witnesses, and make it look like an accident. *General Davis will be resigning and taking a vacation with his family* – Kill General Davis and his entire family, leave no witnesses, make it look like an accident. *It would be good if the Russians met General Davis* – Kill General Davis and make it look like the

Russians did it. *General Davis could say some harmful things* – Lock him up in a prison cell until ordered otherwise.

There was never an exact translation. It was open to interpretation, but when you had worked as long as I had, you had an idea. I only knew that if General Davis had an accidental death, I didn't get a call the next morning.

I could feel the anger building in the pit of my stomach, boiling hatred twisted at my insides. My outward appearance was calm, standing in front of the five board members. I had trained myself to never show physical signs of weakness.

"Mr. Smith, we gave you this position because we felt you were qualified for it," said one of the board members with a flat narrow face. *You failed us you pathetic piece of shit*, my mind translated. The man looked around at his other colleagues for assurance, "The board feels that we might need to make a change of management." · *We are considering slitting your throat, convince us otherwise*, he said. I nodded, placing my hands behind my back.

"Everything is under control. Setbacks happen with every schedule but it will soon be corrected." · *I've got the little bitch in my sights, just back off and let me do my job*, I said. One of the overweight blobs leaned forward, his nose hung awkwardly upon his face like a turkey's red snood.

He said, "The position was comfortable was it not? How can we be sure that you will be cooperative if we continue your employment?" – *How could you fuck up with a secure ambush in a low ventilated building? Why shouldn't we just kill you and find someone else to kill Gothamsreckoning?* I dug my finger hard into the base of my back, my nail ripping at flesh; I could feel the blood begin to drip down my leg.

The voice crept up slow, a subtle whisper to poison my mind. *You will let them win. They will replace you and leave someone else in control. They can't even trust you to kill a woman. What happened to you? Maybe you need a hug or maybe you need some social networking. Disgusting cockroach, they should exterminate you.* I shook awake from my thoughts and came to, a moment or a minute later but the vultures still watched silent. My thumb had managed to make the cut into a gash during my mental absence. Blood was now pooling on the floor behind my right heel.

The flat-faced vulture leaned forward and said, "we feel that we have made a mistake, we won't be..."

"The mistake," I said cutting him off, "is that I decided to come to this room to be lectured by this board. I have served my country faithfully for forty years, and not once have I made a mistake. This world has come to fear my shadow, because when the sun sets, it engulfs the earth and someone goes missing in the night."

"Excuse me?" One of the board members said.

I couldn't hold back anymore, "No, you may not be excused. This country would be sucking on the tit of China if it weren't for men like me. You all sit up there in the sun, exposed and oblivious to the costs of your freedom. You think you know but you don't truly want to know what hides beneath the shadows of these eyes. You've never pressed a father's hands around his seven year old daughter's throat, watching the whole time while her eyes bounce from misunderstanding, to fear, then pain, desperation, and finally acceptance. They seem to give up at a point just before they go blank. The depths of my evil would haunt you. Your worst nightmares are a cute representation of the darkness that we encompass," I said.

The room danced in silence and it was music to my ears. I continued with haste, "This country has been protected by shadows like me for the last two centuries. The things I do for your fucking sunshine..." I paused looking up at them with the sickness plaguing my stomach again. "The sun will set soon and Gothamsreckoning will be dead when it rises and on that day I don't expect to get a fucking phone call." I turned on my heels and walked out revealing the pool of blood at my feet. The board sat silent, not a single whisper heard as I disappeared into the shadows once more.

There was no hiding from the sun in this desert land, stepping off the plane was like being thrown into an oven. Heat swept through my lungs, shocking my system into a coughing fit. Each gasp for air was met with fire that cooked my insides.

Knightcr@wler played the part of a tourist to perfection. Immediately upon arriving, he made us stop at one of those enormous gluttonous truck stops with a horribly cliché name, like Big Boy's Truck Stop, or Sam's Mega One Stop Shop. Include mega, ultra, or big in your gas station's title and the big riggers are sure to come a truckin.

Knightcr@wler was like a kid in a candy store. He ran inside, grabbing enough redneck gear to last to the end of times. It was like he was wearing a disguise before, and we had only seen him as Clark Kent. Now he was in his element, transformed into Possum Hunter, the super hero. He wore fake snakeskin boots, cowboy jeans with fancy designs on the back pockets, a button up denim shirt, a white cowboy hat, and a bandana around his neck. I almost forgot the brown leather fringe gloves because they were so hideous I wanted to forget them. To top it all off, he bought a toy set of silver colt revolvers that were holstered around his waist. They clasped together with a large oval golden belt buckle that said, "I heart Utah."

Knightcr@wler tipped his hat to Kira as he passed and said, "Ma'am. These parts ain't safe for city folk like yaselves. Best be ridin' along." He then waddled to our black SUV, jumped up on the cab step and screamed "YEEHAWWWWW," as he shot one of his pistols in the air. I'll have to give it to him though; the bandanas did help with the dust. I had heard that Utah was diverse in terrain but the west, where we landed, was nothing but vulture heaven.

The drive was long and eventful. We rarely listened to country music and were all trying to memorize the songs and sing along. At any roadside attraction we made it a point to stop and buy at least one trinket or some locally grown produce.

We arrived at the town late in the evening. It felt like one of those ghost towns that you read about or saw in the movies. I halfway expected to see a lone tumbleweed roll across the road or even better a shootout after a heated argument in the local saloon.

The place had a frontier feel to it that I rather enjoyed. It was like I was living in the old Oregon Trail computer game. It gave me a discerning urge to buy up ammunition to hunt and see if there were any nice strong oxen in town worth purchasing.

"Alright, I'll take first watch for the zombie apocalypse," I said starring out the window at our desolate surroundings.

"I'm pretty sure we can easily take on the nine people that live here," Kira said smiling.

Most of the buildings kept their original wooden frames. Some sat with warped wood, slightly dilapidated, but homey all the same. It made me hungry for pancakes, biscuits and gravy, bacon, and eggs from a local diner. Suburban style homes were built not too far in the distance, ruining the main street's quiet quaintness but I tried to ignore them.

At the far end of the strip we saw the Weird Egg Inn. It was hard to miss. The front desk was inside an enormous white egg, and all of the rooms were miniature little eggs with neat hand carved doors that made you think of Easter.

Knightcr@wler jumped out of the car and did his best cowboy swagger up to the lady behind the counter. "Ma'am we got some city folk just roll in, lookin' for a warm bed and a place to get a little night cap." She smiled courteously but her expression settled on displeasure.

"How many rooms?" She asked.

"Well I imagine this little hen and rooster are gonna wanna make some eggs of their own tonight, if you know what I mean." He made a clicking sound with the side of his mouth and tipped his hat to her leaning hard on his right elbow as he probably imagined a southern gentleman would.

Phantom chimed in as well, "yes, also ma'am what temperature do they set their heater on to properly incubate their egg?" This brought a smile to the old ladies face. It sent wrinkles dancing across her weathered cheeks.

I had to jump in before it got out of control, "sorry Ma'am we'll just take two eggs."

They couldn't be stopped at this point and were now just spouting off whatever they could, becoming more and more slap happy with each passing second. "Sunny side up," Phantom cupped his mouth and yelled.

"Ask them if they got any rooms over easy," Knightcr@wler screamed as Kira dragged them both outside.

The woman handed me two separate keys, each attached to a different little chick with a number written on its belly.

Outside, I presented the two hyenas with their key. "Anyone feel like a late breakfast?" I had to ask, it was either the eggs we were standing in front of or the feel of the yesteryears frozen town.

"Hell yes," said Knightcr@wler.

"I couldn't remember why we brought you with us until just now," Phantom said slapping me on the back. There was a diner a couple blocks down and we decided that it was a nice night for a walk.

It was eerie hearing only your footsteps on the way to an establishment. It made all of us a little edgy and I saw Knightcr@wler even do a couple of glances over his shoulder. When it's too quiet in the city it usually means you're in the wrong area at the wrong time.

Dethroned The Wolf came up on the right hand side of the street. Neon red shone brightly off the bar's lettering. The logo was of a wolf's head that had one eye x'd out and the other glowing bright yellow. The glowing eye had a bit of a human quality to it. "Just like the children that turned into wolves that Ender had to drown," Knightcr@wler whispered. I felt my insides buzzing with anticipation, butterflies before the big adventure. We all stared at the wolf as we passed and it felt like its eye was following us.

The diner was called The Desert Moon. The name actually caught me off guard because I liked it. We found a booth near a window that faced the bar and sat down. None of us had had a full meal since we landed so we ordered way too much and a pitcher of beer for the table.

After a couple beers we all became extra friendly, whether or not others wanted to be friendly with us was none of our concern. Still, we all had our mission in mind. The first thing that concerned me was the fact that there were houses right behind the bar. I leaned forward to Knightcr@wler and said, "I thought you said that he owned one hundred yards behind his property?"

"He does, I mean he did….it… it must have been more recent," Knightcr@wler said.

"Well how could they build on the land if there is something underneath it," Phantom said.

"I don't know…." Knightcr@wler said, sounding discouraged for the first time.

"Guys let's not give up before we even walk in," Kira said. "I'd hate to be with you all in the zombie apocalypse…. Bunch of Debbie downers in this group. Another drink bar maid." Kira slammed her beer down on the table.

Phantom was in a separate booth chatting up one of the servers that had been off shift for a good hour. They were giggling and drinking hard, talking in hushed voices.

Kira had a funny look in her eyes after the fourth pitcher and I decided that it was time to call it a night. We parted ways with Phantom and Knightcr@wler. Kira was more than willing, knowing that we would get to spend some much needed alone time in our little egg. She attacked me the moment we got to the room.

I awoke earlier than usual due to the time difference. The egg room was designed so that the top half was semi-transparent letting in a fair amount of natural sunlight. I moved my hands under the sheet like little tentacles until they suctioned upon Kira's smooth bare butt. She gave a soft sigh of pleasure, but kept sleep upon her eyes. Her nipples were erect when I made my way up to them. I slid them between my thumb and middle finger, massaging them in a circular motion. She thrust her butt backwards and began moving it slowly up and down.

Bam.... We both jumped up to the loud noise at the door followed by shrill laughter. Bam, bam, bam, bam, bam, a drum roll of knocks bombarded the door.

"Wakey wakey little chicklings." We heard Phantom say.

"Oh god make them stop," Kira said rolling over, throwing her arm and leg around me. Her squeeze almost took me away from the fact that Phantom and Knightcr@wler were outside the door but then the knocks came again. I ran outside in my boxers opening the door to grab one of them but they both took off and my legs were still sloppy with sleep to catch them. My head pounded with sharp pains from the prior night of drinking. It had been a long while since I had drank so much. Nothing a hot shower couldn't fix though.

It took a bit longer for Kira to get up and rinse off but she finally rose grunting like a primal savage. She hated mornings and was capable of sleeping all day if she was allowed. Some funny noises came from the shower that sounded like throwing up but I couldn't tell for sure and kissed her all the same.

It was a little past eight in the morning and it was already too hot for my liking. We were all sweating profusely by the time we finished the short walk to the bar.

It was a funny feeling to be heading to a bar to hydrate. I felt like an alcoholic for the first time in my life.

As the door swung open the wolf logo let out a long disturbing growl that Kira only laughed at. "Sounds like the winner you took home last night Phantom," she said.

"You bastard," Phantom said smiling. "I was only gathering intel. She told me that those two houses on the property were there when it was revealed and the people that live in them have to pay next to nothing for rent. Almost as if they were free."

That perked up Knightcr@wler's attention, "I knew it!" he said.

The bar was dim lit and the bartender was wiping down glasses as we entered. I had always wanted to see a bartender doing that. It was like the stereotypical bartender thing to do in almost all video games and movies. There were tables that seated four all along the west wall and the bar took up most of the east wall with typical bar stools surrounding it. Near the back were toilets, a bookshelf, pool table, a long mirror, and a cocktail table arcade game.

The long mirror was the first thing that caught my eye because it had a golden snake wrapped around the entirety of its frame. In the book the snake would uncoil itself from the rug and attack Ender in the castle beyond the end of the world. Ender defeated the snake by kissing it on accident, or so he thinks.

Phantom ordered us all waters as Kira, Knightcr@wler, and I made our way over to the mirror for a closer look. In an instant though our focus changed from the mirror to the arcade game. We saw the confirmation we had been waiting for, knowing that we were on the right track. An Ender's

Game cocktail table arcade game sat in front of us. I had never seen a single Ender's Game video arcade, and with a quick google search I confirmed that no one had ever created one. Ender was on the side of it in his battle school suit, holding a gun in his hands while screaming commands at soldiers pouring in around him from an octagon gate.

"Phantom, come look at this," Knightcr@wler called out. Phantom downed the entire cup of water, asked for a refill, and made his way over. His eyes, once barely open, were now wide with disbelief.

"I never knew they made a game?" Phantom said.

"They didn't," Knightcr@wler said smiling. "Bartender," Knightcr@wler waved his hand over at him as if there were others at the bar that he had to steal his attention from. "Could I please get two dollars worth of quarters?" he said placing two dollars on the freshly cleaned glistening bar. The man grabbed the two dollars, fumbled through the cash register and gave him a stack of quarters.

Knightcr@wler came over, half skipping with a big grin on his face. Our eyes were glued to the opening credits as Knightcr@wler tossed the quarter into the slit marked in red with 25¢. The coin passed through entirely rattling its way down into the return slot. Phantom picked it up again but this time he put it in the second slit yet was awarded with the same results.

"Machine doesn't accept coins." The bartender said cleaning another pint glass around its rim.

"Why did you give me the quarters then?" Knightcr@wler said visibly annoyed.

"Thought you might have wanted to play pool. Not too many people come to a bar at eight in the morning to play video games," the bartender said.

"Touche good sir, Touche," Knightcr@wler said.

"Give me your money and I'll get you the credits," the bartender called out. "I'll take three dollars' worth." Knightcr@wler said giving the man three crisp dollar bills from his billfold.

"You don't want to give me back the quarters?" The bartender called out from the register.

"The day is yet young and we have lots of drinking to do. We might play a hundred games of quarters for all I know." Knightcr@wler said. The bartender smiled and put the money in the cash register.

"The game only goes up to nine credits but I'll give you the other three when you lose a couple." The bartender said grabbing a key and making his way around the bar over to the game. He inserted the key into the front panel where the coin slits were and opened it to reveal the chaotic interior of twisted wiring. There was a lever on the back side that he clicked nine times and the credits came chiming in with a voice saying the first syllable of Ender eight times like some sort of glitch until the ninth credit rang out, "Ender Wiggin welcome to battle school!" The screen started dancing to life.

The game's controls were a little advanced with knobs here and there as well as a roller ball. It also had the standard joystick along with eight multicolor buttons. The controls made you feel like you were about to man an aircraft. Knightcr@wler was the first to try because he had brought us here and by right, he could play as long as he wanted.

The game started him out as Ender Wiggin in first person view. The graphics were pretty pixilated but futuristic in a way. It was like a little more in depth version of Minecraft. Knightcr@wler ran around a bit with Ender, running into mostly restricted areas until he found the game room where other battle school students were huddled around different arcade games. Knightcr@wler already knew which one to go toward immediately.

The older boys crowded around a holograph game where ships were battling each other virtually in midair. He challenged one of the boys to the game. The older kids made jests but finally let him in to play. "This is just like the book," said Knightcr@wler.

The game was a heads up dogfight, ship against ship. You could set traps to try and trick the enemy that was following you. You had mines, drifting bombs and then maneuvers like Star Fox in Nintendo 64 where you could loop around behind them or barrel roll. Knightcr@wler lost the first match pretty quickly. "We have to do it exactly like the book. Best two out of three. Ender loses the first match and wins the second two," said Knightcr@wler, zoned into the game.

"Yeah right newbie," said Phantom and it made Knightcr@wler smile because the other boys in the video game were now laying into him as well in their battle school slang. Phantom and I picked up on it quick, taunting him with every move, "You nothin, you ain't mo than poop from you butt," Phantom said.

"You lose one mo gain and you be iced launchie," I added. Knightcr@wler was almost laughing too much to control but he was a pro and contained himself to win the second and third match with ease.

The game was actually much easier than we thought it would be. He really was just letting the other boy win the first time. A message popped up on the screen with a one up sound instructing Ender to report to his quarters. Knightcr@wler ran around for a bit and then found the barracks and went to Ender's locker where another message popped up saying Rabbit Army at 14:00 hours. He got into his flash suit, grabbed his gun and headed toward the null gravity battle room.

The battle room was where the game really began. Ender had command of forty-five players that he could group into toons or use them solo. Toons were comprised of five to eight boys. The game was all in real time so you had to micro manage a lot. Each player had a freeze gun that froze whatever part of the body they shot. If you shot them in the chest it froze their entire body but until that happened the player was free to move whatever unfrozen limbs they had.

The battle arena was different every game, but there were certain constants. Every battle took place in a null gravity three-dimensional hexagon environment. There were almost always stationary stars scattered throughout the space. Stars were solid objects that could be used as a tactical advantage or as an obstacle. The two army's gates open on opposite sides of the battlegrounds and the game begins. To win, one must either freeze all of the opposing team's players with their freeze guns or have four unfrozen players place themselves on the four sides of the gate to open it for a fifth player to fly through. If the fifth entered the enemy gate unfrozen, then the game was over and their team won.

At the start, Knightcr@wler created nine toons out of his forty-five members with five players in each toon. You could launch the toons in any direction you wanted but you would have to switch from toon to toon to control them. If you put them on auto control they did nothing inventive and just shot at the other army with base level artificial intelligence. When they collided with a wall they bounced off as an inanimate object would, controlled by their own inertia. To avoid that, you had to control everything at once.

It had been too many years since Knightcr@wler had played physical computer games where micro managing strategies were key to victory and his inexperience showed. His toons bounced off the walls carelessly and were frozen by the computers team with ease. He over extended himself and didn't have time to jump back and forth between each toon before they got into trouble. Once he got down to three toons his strategy kicked back in but by then, the other team tore him to pieces with strength in numbers and formations. Knightcr@wler went through five credits without winning a single battle before he gave up.

Phantom jumped in to try his hand at the controls, taking a different approach. He decided to throw out the notion of creating toons, only sending single players in one at a time in different directions. He sent four along the sides of each of the walls but not after sending three in a rotating formation down the center. The computer didn't know what to make of it and sent too many toons at the decoy group. The four players he sent along the outside walls attacked from behind them freezing multiple opponents before getting frozen themselves and Phantom had others already pouring in to attack them from the front while they focused on protecting their rear. It was a beautiful strategy and won him a commanding victory over the Rabbit army.

The next battle was against Rat army. Phantom attempted the same strategy but the computer reacted like artificial intelligence, learning it and adapting accordingly. Rat army crushed him in a matter of minutes. He sat back, dumb founded.

I pushed Phantom aside and took control. When my gate opened I could see a cube design with stars on each of its corners floating in the center of the arena. I sent a toon of five to each of the four stars closest to my gate. The computer in turn did the same. It was attempting to mimic my strategy, was my initial thought so I gave it something it had seen before. I sent the same formation that Phantom did just minutes before. My players were gliding along the four outer walls while a group of three spiraled down the center but this time when they reacted to the strategy they had seen before, I sent my four toons out from behind the stars to directly behind the stars that they had control of. While they scrambled to shoot the players from the center and the rear I sent the five players huddled behind each star over to attack from every angle. It worked even with the enemy trying to counter with toons pouring out from their own gate. Once I commanded control of all eight of the stars it became target practice.

I was able to outsmart the computer by using tricks that Ender used for the next three battles, bringing me victory against Phoenix, Leopard, and Badger army. The AI was only susceptible to surprise strategies once. "The computer is like water," I said in my best sounding Bruce Lee voice. "It is shapeless, formless, like water. When you pour water in a cup it becomes the cup. When you pour water in a bottle, it becomes the bottle. When you pour water in a teapot, it becomes the teapot. Water can drip and it can crash.

Become like water my friend. Be water." Kira smiled and rubbed my back as I focused on the next battle against two armies.

"This must be the final battle," Knightcr@wler said. "Well as long as it follows the book." I was matched against Griffin and Tiger Army. I tried the formation that Ender used in the book to sneak five players to the gate but the computer saw it coming and destroyed me. Next match I tried to use stars as tactical positions but the overwhelming numbers of the two armies combined overtook me with ease. I let Kira jump in to give it a try. She had flawless strategies and won position here and there but eventually was overcome by the sheer numbers as well.

At that point we had the bartender give us more credits. We paid a bit more money to bring us back up to nine and Knightcr@wler took back the controls. He sent his nine different toons of five in every direction trying to sneak attack the gate with one of them but the computer had formations surrounding the gate as if it expected that strategy every time. Knightcr@wler gave up after another four tries. Phantom gave up after one. When I took back over I tried with the best strategy that I could think of. It failed just as the others did. "This level is impossible," said Knightcr@wler.

"We noob. We ain't but spit on yo shoe," said Phantom in the battle school slang.

"Someone keep trying," Kira said as she walked over to the bartender to order. Knightcr@wler sat back down and started zoning in again.

Kira ordered everything on the menu at the bar as well as eight pitchers of water. By about two in the afternoon we were all close to fully recovered. We had gone through twenty dollars in quarters when the bartender said "you know the game's rigged right? I've seen people spend months trying to beat that level. I even bought the book one time and used every strategy Ender ever used in battle and it's impossible."

"Well then, I guess it's time to start thinking outside the box. Four pitchers of your finest cheap beer on draught sir," Kira said smiling.

Phantom looked as if he was going to puke after the first drink but he soldiered through and by three in the afternoon we were buzzed and back at the game. Knightcr@wler was sending his players to the back of the stars and then gripping one by the arm and leg, to hurl them around a star at lightning speed only to have them bounce off the wall. He was laughing maniacally as their bodies went limp after the collision.

"Wait, that's it!" I said.

"What's it?" Knightcr@wler said half paying attention to me.

"Look, Ender wanted to win at any cost, right?" I said.

"Of course," Knightcr@wler said as if it was common knowledge.

"Right now we are playing the game, the game that was created by the computer and we are outmatched. So let's not play the game like they want us to. Hurt them!" I said looking at everyone like they would understand right away. They looked at me like I had gone mental. "Here, let me take over," I said. Knightcr@wler moved aside and let me on the controls.

I split my army into two groups, giving half of the soldiers weapons to the other half, making one group unarmed and the other duel wielding. "Look for Ender to get to the End of the World door, he had to kill each of the children so they wouldn't turn into wolves. After he killed them he dragged them into the river to drown them to ensure that they wouldn't return. Most of Enders most decisive victories were vicious. To get to the End of the World we need to drown these children. Well drown them metaphorically."

I sent the unarmed half of my army behind the star closest to my gate. Then I made a chain out of the players by having them grip each other's hands to the next ones legs. Once the connection was made I froze their hands in place so that their flash suit wouldn't let them release their grip and they became locked in place. I froze three at the end of the chain to form a sort of human wrecking ball and then the fun began.

I launched the frozen students around the star toward the central mass of the enemy. With the centripetal force, the human wrecking ball was soaring toward them at a lethal speed. It crashed into the enemy sending blood flying in every direction. The game amplified the damage and made it so that limbs were being torn from body. The enemy became children again and some of their team started to panic. Even though my human wrecking ball was filled with frozen players, it only needed four unfrozen players to control it. Any enemy that wasn't killed by the wrecking ball was shot by the other half of my army, now pouring through the gate with duel freeze guns. It only took a couple minutes before the match was over.

Kira, Knightcr@wler, and Phantom all squeezed me tight while keeping one avid eye on the game to see what would happen. Stars started zooming past the screen and then the word "CONGRATULATIONS" centered itself in the monitor and a voice started to speak, "Ender Wiggin! Congratulations, you have completed battle school." Then the screen glitched and reset.

Knightcr@wler hit the side of the game instinctively "What?" There was nothing, no clue, no big ending, just a blank screen. The bartender even looked surprised.

"We've got to get that game removed. Sorry guys. If you want I can give you guys a couple free pitchers for being the first to beat that stupid game. Thing's been in here ever since the place opened. Owner won't let the damn thing go."

Knightcr@wler's face went blank, "nothing, not even a whisper of a clue. It's a dead end..."

Chapter 17: On the Road
Source: Journal
Name: Mark Boggs

My seat hummed a sweet lullaby to the engine's vibrations, purring my body into a slumber. I was half awake or half asleep, day tripping in between worlds that played tricks on my putty like mind.

Silvia was driving the diesel-powered car and I glanced over at her from time to time trying to make sense of the emotions that gripped at me. Some civil war was being waged inside, that my mind wasn't capable of dealing with. Sally grabbed my cold hands and blew hard to warm them up. I hadn't noticed but they were shaking profusely and soft purples and blues painted my palms. She was rubbing them in between hers, a trick that I taught her to keep her own hands warm when she was younger. Her small little fingers turned so white in the winter.

Silvia looked over and her hand lashed out at the heater like a viper cranking it up to full blast. "My god! I'm sorry. I... I didn't even notice. I was lost in..." she trailed off.

"Thought... yeah..." I said understanding exactly what she meant. The heat slipped through my collar and sleeves, sliding along my legs, caressing my bare skin with warmth.

Within the hour Bell and Sally were asleep in the back. "Gothamsreckoning," I said smiling for some reason, like some sick joke had been played on me that I just now understood.

"I know…" she said sighing. "Believe me, I didn't pick the name. It just… found me… Kind of fitting now though don't you think?" she said.

"Yeah, it has the whole vigilante ring to it," I replied. "So you were Gothamsreckoning all along," I said shaking my head.

"I wanted to tell you… I didn't know if… I guess I've grown a little guarded," she said stumbling around like a shy teenager. I began laughing out loud. "What?" she said flinging her hair from her eyes so she could see me fully.

"You know you were supposed to be my big payday… Well, now that that's out… how much does revolting against the government pay?" I said. She looked at me and smiled. She then turned back to the road and focused.

Bell began coughing and wheezing a bit in the back seat and Silvia's eyes flared with concern. It only lasted a second but I could see the motherly instinct take hold. I didn't want to pry but I had to know. "Where's Bell's father?"

Silvia turned sharply to look in Bell's direction only to find her deep in sleep. Her shoulders relaxed a bit and she talked soft, "I had been on the run for so long. It felt like a nightmare that I couldn't wake up from. Trust was a fairytale that rich parents read to warm plump children on cold nights. I was trained and molded to survive, to hide among the places that society had left to rot and die in the shadows. I built my empire in the darkness, waiting for a moment to be able to present myself… I remember I used to watch the movie Terminator 2 and think of myself as John Connor leading the revolution. It gave me hope when I was deceived; it gave me strength when I was tortured. I learned to stop trusting people, to turn off emotions, to die inside… that's when I found Bell."

Silvia looked back again to make sure she was still sleeping. "She was so tiny and innocent. A perfect baby girl wrapped in a rich white woven blanket with a pink floral trim." Silvia's eyes began to water. "This perfect little angel was everything I had never known. She sat silent and wide-eyed and innocent. Her eyes were filled with life and hope. I envied her. For a moment I hated her... mainly because she made me hate myself. Blood stained dumpsters and broken glass surrounded this perfect baby girl and for a second I thought... *leave her.* I mean, I wasn't but a child myself and I was so cold and calculated that here sat life in front of me and I was thinking about what a helpless burden she would be. A burden... Can you believe that?" I sat motionless knowing that it was a rhetorical question.

Silvia began crying and I rubbed her back trying to comfort her. She cleared her throat and began again. "I turned to leave and then it happened. She laughed. Right then and there something changed in me. I knew I couldn't leave her there. I knew that I couldn't let that darkness engulf her. I promised myself that I would raise her to believe in fairytales and prince charming, the grass on the other side of the hill and heaven. I had let myself die inside and I didn't want the same fate for that innocent little child." She began smiling now. "Then the funniest thing happened. She saved me. Her belief in the just and good revived me. She breathed life back into chambers that I had forgotten and locked away. She was my key to salvation. I am nothing without her. I don't want to remember what my life was like before her. I don't know what happened to her mother and father but I saw the blood. There is still a sick part of me that is thankful for what happened to the parents. Some selfish part of me that lives in the last bits of darkness left in my soul... the part that is a survivor and will survive whether I want it to or not."

She wasn't sick. She was human. I knew of the selfish demons that plagued us all and mine was delighted in the fact that she had never had a husband. This woman just poured her soul out to me and I was only concerned with the idea that she had never had a child with another man and maybe even hadn't been in love before. I knew it was sick but something about being the only man in a woman's life was comforting. I shook my head bringing myself back to the moment at hand.

There was nothing I could say that would help her in this situation. I just sat silent, consumed with my own thoughts. She was so strong. I could see strength coursing through her veins.

The car hit a bump on the road and we swerved just enough to wake Bell up. "Mom, are we almost there?" She said.

"A couple more hours honey." She rubbed her eyes and climbed over the center console and into my lap. She was wearing Minnie Mouse pajamas that draped off of her wrists like a sorcerer's cloak. I instinctively put her under my seatbelt and wrapped my arms around her for protection. Bell placed her arms under my own so that it looked like mine were her abnormally large arms and then began going, "RAWRRRR," like some sort of dinosaur waving them back and forth.

She giggled and smiled looking up at me to see if I thought she was funny as well. My lips curled up and that was all she needed. She then turned my hand over and started singing little songs while dancing her fingers down the cracks in my rough palms.

My conscience weaved in out of reality as I looked out the window. "Your hands are rough compared to my mom's... I bet..." her voice faded out and the trees blurred into a barrage of pastels. Dull yellows, warm reds, and amber oranges brushed against my window. I don't know how long I was out but when I came to, Bell was sleeping, her head resting against my chest, rising and falling with each breath.

I had been sweating profusely but luckily Bell was dry. She looked like an angel cuddled up on my lap. "She likes you a lot," Silvia said, her voice a mouse like whisper. "I have never seen her take to someone so freely. You are her shining knight." Silvia paused for a long while but I could tell something wanted to escape her throat. "You know... That night that you rescued her." She stopped again, but continued to force more out. "That was where I found her. Somehow she knows it... She sneaks off there sometimes. If you wouldn't have been there..." She could barely speak at this point and I could hear her getting choked up but she pushed it back down. "I never got to thank you for what you did," she said.

"I thought your thanks was the torture." I said. She laughed out loud at that one.

"Oh gosh..." she let out a relieved sigh. "I remember thinking how funny you were even on the verge of being beaten to death. I'm glad you hunted me." Right then her focus changed. "Shoot, running really low on gas. Let's get off the highway and refuel."

She took the next exit and traveled a quarter of a mile down a dirt road surrounded by thick woods. The car kicked up dust in its wake that spun around in turbine like dust devils. She turned the engine off and we went to work on getting the fuel cans out of the trunk.

Silvia was pouring the third five-gallon drum into the tank when I heard something off in the woods. It startled me so much that I grabbed Bell by the waist, picking her up and placing her safely on the opposite side of my body. I crouched down and moved my focus in and out of the depths of the brush. Then I saw it out in the distance, an enormous buck, its antlers glistening in the sun as it strode through the thick woods like a king. I placed my hand over Bell's mouth and I pointed the direction of the animal out to her. She struggled at first but then went tense when her eyes locked onto it. She was mesmerized and I could feel her heartbeat racing with excitement.

I had forgotten the wonder that animals brought at that age. It had been so long since I myself had seen a wild animal. "What is it doing?" Bell said as quiet as she could. The buck spun his head in our direction and perked its ears up at attention. It waited for a while and then dipped its head down. Just then a beautiful doe came out from behind him as if she was given the all-clear signal, followed by a fawn. "It's a family!" Bell was getting so excited that she could hardly contain herself. "Can we pet them?" I shook my head no. I pointed at my eyes and signaled for her just to watch. I was almost at her height and was able to speak to Bell on a more intimate level.

"When I was your age, they used to keep wild animals in Zoos and Aquariums. We took babies just like that one from their mother and father and raised them in cages twice the size of our car. We didn't know the things that we know now." Bell looked up at me with her big pupils. They looked like portals that were open for impression.

"What do we know now?" She asked.

"That animals are meant to be free just as we are. That they are more like us than we ever used to give them credit for. They are meant to have families, love, grow old, roam, and dream." Bell turned back to the family and watched but with a smile on her face now.

I had to give it to Charles, VEG really did change the face of the earth for more than just people. He made augmented reality so realistic that Zoos and Aquariums could stay open without imprisoning animals. Once films like Black Fish, The Cove, and other controversial documentaries came out about the mistreatment of animals the people rallied for their freedom.

Charles took it upon himself to revolutionize Zoos and Aquariums. He saw that the animals were mistreated and lonely. That they lived sad existences, and even if they wanted to give up and die we kept them alive with medicine, force-feeding them to make sure they paid off what they were worth in entertainment value.

He teamed up with the best robotics specialists and engineers in the world to create life-like renditions of every animal you could think of that children could interact with. He used architectural programs to put kids swimming underwater with a school of whales or dolphins, flying with eagles, and running with cheetahs. Museums became so interactive and fun that they saw more profit than they had ever had with actual animals. There wasn't food or medical expenses other than for animal rehabilitation. They brought back the true animal lover employees again and we took another "giant leap for mankind."

People could still pay to go down and swim with the whales in Central America, but they were in natural habitats that the whales chose for introduction. They knew that their kin would be exposed to humans at some point, so they wanted to teach them who we are at an early age.

The difference with these introduction environments was the animal has the choice to visit. They are free. There was no coaxing or enticing with food to domesticate. It was their choice, and some people would spend months down in Central America without seeing a single whale.

Charles had the ability to see our potential greatness. He always quoted Stephen Hawking's ideas on Aliens in interviews. Every time he freed captive animals, rehabilitating them into the wild, he would say, "If aliens ever come down to earth, we only have to look at ourselves to see how intelligent life might develop into something we wouldn't want to meet." Then he goes on to say, "How can we expect aliens to treat us with compassion when we treat animals that we feel are inferior like this?"

VROOOMMMMMMMM the car roared as its engine started. The family of deer jumped with fright, all running in the same direction at lightning speed. "Mom!" Bell turned around screaming. Silvia hopped out of the car oblivious to the moment we just had.

"Time to get going," she said slapping the roof of the muscle car. Bell sighed and grabbed me by the hand, guiding me to the car. She was obedient, the complete opposite of her mother. I loved them both.

Chapter 18: New Day
Source: Personal Computer Log
Name: Mr. Smith
Location: Penthouse Apartment

I woke up face down, naked and bare, my penis erect and throbbing as I thrust it into my Flokati blanket. Tentacle-like sheep hairs were dancing around the tip of my prick and I loved it. The sun sent ripples of soft blues rolling over my pillow as it rose into position behind the fish tank covering the entirety of my penthouse's east facing wall.

Bloodthirsty Piranhas swam back and forth eyeing me with disgust. They hadn't been fed in two days, and I delighted in their hatred of me. Their hungry eyes excited my sexual urges. I jumped to my feet, yelling for my maid, "Merriam". She came in hastily wearing a tight white outfit that her young busty breasts almost broke free of.

Seeing me nude and erect didn't faze her at this point. At my bedside drawer, she squeezed lotion onto both of her hands grabbing two tissues before approaching. She started with my testicles, her long red nails tickling in a delicate manner, grazing my cock periodically. Then slid smooth up to my shaft teasing it a bit before going to work.

I didn't need much foreplay this time. She started whispering complements to my member as she stroked it repeatedly. "Silence," I scolded her. I wasn't in the mood for talk. "My glove, and be quick about it. If I go soft while you rummage through my belongings you'll wish you had never come to America." She was gone and back again within a couple seconds barely missing a stroke.

My penis was now tingling, twitching with each touch. She placed the glove on my right hand. It was made from a heavy rubber and laced with metal chain mesh, a spike protruding from the thumb and forefinger.

I approached the piranha tank and worked in a methodical fashion. Pricking my left forefinger, I poured a couple drops of blood into the tank's feeding hole. This sent the piranhas into frenzy. My cock was feeling so good that I could prematurely blow before the act. Merriam was beating away furiously now, after seeing my leg begin to quiver.

I reached my gloved hand into the hostile waters and the piranhas jumped at it biting viciously. One was braver than the rest, not retreating, most likely the alpha. It just sat there hovering around my hand, biting it over and over again until I clenched my thumb and forefinger hard. The two metal spikes pierced through its temples killing him instantly. My penis began to spasm shooting my load all over the glass of the tank while blood poured out of the Piranha's puncture wounds. It expelled outwards, a red cloud engulfing the once clear waters. I ripped the fish out of the tank and threw it in a bowl resting next to it. "Fillet it and serve it with a glass of Sauvignon Blanc in thirty minutes. I'll be in the shower washing up." I walked away, while she wiped down the glass and grabbed the bowl to head toward the kitchen.

After a hot shower I slipped into my Brioni suit, steam still pouring off my body. It was tailored to perfection. On great mornings I indulged a little. I placed a fresh Casa Fuente cigar in my suit pocket and strolled into the kitchen where my breakfast awaited.

A crisp New York Times was folded and placed next to my Sauvignon Blanc. Most men had transitioned to reading their paper on tablets or VEG, but call me old fashion I felt it lacked the class. The smell of a fresh newspaper was intoxicating. The ink poured off the pages and awakened my senses. It was as if a woman laid before me, new and unique, the chase if you will. I begin learning her intricacies with the turn of each page, until I learn all there is to know, which is when my favorite part comes. I've lost interest, figured her out, and now get to discard her to the trash.

I loved being alone in my penthouse. People who get bored disgust me. The ones that have to voice their boredom deserved to die in my book. It displays a weak mind and a terrible personality. You have an infinitesimal amount of wonders to ponder within your brain yet you find the ability not to use it. Merriam understood my joy of seclusion and knew to never be present in the same room unless I called upon her. My cell phone broke my train of thoughts, vibrating loudly next to my fork. A text popped up on the screen reading, "Number 5 detained awaiting your presence." Change hummed in the air, and I felt optimistic for the first time in years. I gathered my things, took a deep swig of my Sauvignon Blanc and headed for the door.

Chapter 19: The End of the World
Time: Five Years Prior
Source: Personal Computer Log
User: Evo

We were there when the bar opened, we were there through the so-called "local rush" and it looked as though we were going to be there when it closed. Knightcr@wler had beaten the game a total of ten times at this point hoping that it was just a glitch. He even had the bartender check for faulty wiring, but neither of them really knew what they were looking for. Phantom was busy looking around the bar with his VEG Jacks, but there was nothing. We had all checked it out earlier but Phantom seemed convinced that we were missing something.

Kira was getting drunk. Her and Knightcr@wler were playing Super Nintendo Tennis. One person served up a letter and then they went back and forth naming Super Nintendo games that started with that letter until one of them couldn't name one. The person that couldn't would lose the point.

Knightcr@wler had crushed her in original Nintendo games but in Super Nintendo Kira was up forty to fifteen. They were currently on the letter E and Kira had just named E.V.O. as her hit. Knightcr@wler was drawing a blank. He was spinning a quarter on the table, trying to think of another game. "That's time," Kira said.

"It's only been two minutes. On the last match I gave you like half an hour on the final point," Knightcr@wler said.

"Here," Kira said, slamming the quarter down with her hand. "You get one spin and three flicks to keep it spinning as long as you can. Once it falls, after the third flick, your time's up." Knightcr@wler loved the wager because he loved spinning quarters. He pinned the quarter vertically under his left pointer finger. Then flicked it hard across its side, sending it spinning toward the center of the glazed wooden tabletop. The quarter was a blur of silver; he leaned back and took no notice of it as he thought.

"Who serves up an E? You're so cheap Kira. There are only two freaking games that start with an E, Earth Worm Jim and E.V.O. The only reason you knew EVO is because of your lover." He leaned forward again and used his first flick to send the quarter spinning back to the center.

"YEAH," the bartender yelled clapping at the TV screen. The Red Sox had just gotten a home run against the Yankees, and Knightcr@wler turned back to Kira with his eyes wide open, "EXTRA INNINGS!" he screamed with excitement. He tossed the quarter to Kira "Same deal, five flicks, suck it Kira."

She smiled and said, "I only need one." She flicked the quarter hard and it spun for a second before flying off the table. "EarthBound."

"EarthBound? I've never heard of EarthBound. Challenge," Knightcr@wler said.

Challenges were allowed once per match when someone was thought to be cheating. "Well then obviously you didn't play too many RPG's growing up," Kira said.

"Whatever I challenge," he insisted. They both looked at me since I was the mediator and was allowed access to VEG.

I confirmed the answer was correct and gave him a brief history of the game that I knew would only enrage him more.

Then Kira put the icing on the cake, "Game, Set, Match... Losers go fetch."

Knightcr@wler got up and began looking for the quarter that had fallen underneath the adjacent table somewhere. "GUYS," Knightcr@wler shouted from somewhere beneath us. "Get down here quick." Kira and I both went crawling to where Knightcr@wler was crouched, focusing on something. "How many tables are there?" he said with his thumb and pointer finger wrapped around the base of the leg.

"What? Why?" I asked.

"Just count the tables real quick," He said, focused on something. I stood up and took a quick glance.

"Seven," I said crouching back down for a better look.

The design at the very bottom of the leg was flames climbing up. It looked like a part of the woodcarving but as I looked along the rest of the tables I noticed that each leg was different. "I can move it," Knightcr@wler said as he shifted, twisting the base of the leg to the right. There was a soft clicking sound and then a secret wooden compartment shot outwards toward Kira. It had a simple rotating combination dial on it that had the numbers zero through seven. "This is fire. Fire must represent Dragon army. It can't be by ranking because Orson Scott doesn't discuss the ranking in detail," Knightcr@wler said as he turned the dial slowly. "It must be by order in the book. Ender never fought Dragon army because he was on Dragon but he was in three other teams first. Regardless dragon must be zero." He moved the dial into place and nothing happened. Kira pushed the compartment back in and then the flames on the design lit up red.

"It's a code!" said Knightcr@wler. Kira slapped her hand over Knightcr@wler's mouth. His eyes were wild with excitement and now flushed with a mixture of anger. Kira made a hand motion toward the bartender who was still enthralled with the baseball game. Knightcr@wler slowly shifted his head up and down with acknowledgement. Kira was right, this was not the time to reveal a hidden door inside a bar. Knightcr@wler shifted the table's leg back to pop out the compartment and then rotated the number to six before pushing it back into place. We all got up as if nothing had happened. I grabbed Phantom, we paid the tab, and walked out.

We were going to wait till the bar closed at one in the morning but we had a bit of luck. Since the bar was dead, they closed just a little after midnight. "Wait so we are going to break the law to complete a VEG quest?" Phantom asked.

"Charles Sanders owns this bar. We can't get arrested for completing a quest that he built these structures for." Knightcr@wler said. Phantom was in agreement.

"There has to be some kind of way to get in though without breaking a window or picking a lock," Kira said.

I put my Jacks on and saw it immediately. A giant augmented neon sign said "Late Night Entrance This Way" pointing at a window in the back. "Look guys!" I took some quick snap shots and displayed it on the ground in front of us with the projector function on my frames since only Phantom had his Jacks.

"Good find baby," Kira said, patting my bottom as we walked toward the window.

The window opened with ease and there was a ledge that made climbing inside rather easy. "I don't know how this place hasn't been robbed blind," Phantom said.

"I think I found my new favorite bar," Knightcr@wler said. Once inside it was all business. "Bring up the book in your Jacks Evo," Knightcr@wler said. He was breathing heavy and you could hear the excitement in his voice. I was already on top of it and was doing quick searches for keywords throughout the book with correlation to their page number.

Knightcr@wler had already activated the first leg of the Dragon Army table. "Alright, Ender started on Salamander army," I said.

Knightcr@wler got up and went toward the next table "We know, we know... which armies did he fight?" Knightcr@wler sounded annoyed.

"Condor and Leopard army. Then he went to Rat army and Centipede is the only army name mentioned. Next he was with Phoenix but it doesn't give a specific battle. When Graff gives him Dragon army he fought... Hold on... Six different armies. That's got to be it. Dragon is Zero and the others are the one through six, making seven tables!" I said.

Kira and Phantom were both going toward their own tables. "I've got fire with what looks like wings over here," said Kira.

"Ok good. That's Phoenix, number two," I said looking over the order again and bringing it up in an augmented space in front of me. Kira performed the same actions she had seen Knightcr@wler do hours before and within a few seconds the designs on the legs of her table were glowing as well.

"I got Badger over here," said Phantom.

"Number 4," I yelled.

.We had three tables glowing now. Knightcr@wler lit up Rabbit without even asking. He had studied the book way too much.

"What is this one?" Kira said.

Knightcr@wler was across the room in an instant. "Salamander," he said as he rotated it to number three. "That was the fight where they were allowed access to the battle arena twenty minutes before Ender. They hung against the outside of Ender's gate. God, Bonzo was total noob," Knightcr@wler said.

"Alright I got stripes over here," said Phantom.

"That's five or six try one or the other," I said.

"No, try five. Make them both five. The last table is Griffin. Ender fought Tiger and Griffin army at the same time. There won't be a six. It's just a little trick."

Knightcr@wler said. "He's right," said Phantom when the tiger table started glowing.

Knightcr@wler did the honors of the last table, pushing the compartment back in to watch the final one come to life. Without warning, the snake that was wrapped around the mirror opened its mouth. There was a hissing sound followed by smoke that poured from his mouth, filling the entire room with a blinding fog. The snake's eyes were the only thing visible, red and ominous, sending lazars through the dense fog that both landed somewhere underneath the bar. A tiny secret compartment slid out with a metallic hum and a contrasted bright light shot up from its interior.

Once the smoke cleared, we made our way over to the spectacle. Inside the silver compartment, bathed in white light, was a golden coin. It looked like it had a battle school logo on it. Knightcr@wler picked it up and twirled it round and round with his fingers as I snapped pictures of it. His eyes lit up and without speaking he ran over to the arcade game he had beaten so many times before, tossing the golden coin into the twenty-five cent slot. This time the machine didn't reject the coin but accepted it and one credit appeared with the exhilarating, "Ender Wiggin, Welcome to Battle School."

Knightcr@wler played through the entire game with ease since he had already beaten it a thousand times. It felt like none of us were breathing, all eyes were fixated on the game, and an eerie silence hung on the air. When the victory theme sounded the stars came flying by and the word "Congratulations" came into the center of the screen just like before. This time the glitch brought change. The screen looked like it had rebooted, going into DOS mode and it began ghost typing in ancient programming font:

```
What do you seek in Dethroned the Wolf?

I seek _____
```

A keyboard came up in the display. Knightcr@wler had already known the answer since he started us on this quest and he typed it in letter by letter.

The screen went blank. Nothing happened and Knightcr@wler slammed his head down against the video monitor, "not again....." Suddenly, the floor started vibrating and the entire cocktail arcade cabinet along with a good bit of the floor around it began rising up.

Knightcr@wler's body shifted as he yanked his head off the table. He tried to get up but his foot got caught on the leg of the chair sending him falling backwards off the rising platform. He crawled back, like it was some kind of alien revealing itself. Kira, Phantom, and I began stepping away as the cabinet climbed higher and higher toward the ceiling. When it finally stopped an entire stairwell was revealed leading downward into the darkness, smoke pouring out of it like a dragon's nostrils. We found it. We found the entrance to Charles Sanders most prized quest and it was within five feet of us.

The room was void of solace; the walls bare brick with a stereotypical stainless steel table centered in the room. The man was visibly nervous, sweating profusely as he fidgeted in his pocket. He pulled out a pack of smokes. "Do you mind?" he asked.

"No not at all," I said while I looked over his file. "In fact, I might join you."

I pulled the cigar from my inside jacket pocket. It was smooth and long, Winston Churchill style. The man was still fumbling around his pocket for a light. He groped himself wildly searching with desperation.

"Allow me." I said smiling warmly while taking my case of black matches out. His cigarette shifted in his mouth from the appreciative grin he gave as fire engulfed the tip. He inhaled slowly, a wave of calmness swept over him, "Is there a reason you were so nervous a moment ago Mr. Miller?" I said while lighting my cigar, turning it back and forth, puffing slow until the end's cherry was bright red.

"I've just heard that the heads of your operations don't... don't last long sir. But... I'm greatly honored by the opportunity and I won't let you down." He said.

The Casa Fuente cigar had now bathed me in sweet smoke. It barged into every inch of the room overtaking the cigarette's cheap odor, until only it existed. "It says here that you have no wife or children?"

"Yes sir, women don't love a workaholic," he said.

"Or an alcoholic, for that matter," I chimed in. "Says here you've been given multiple citations for drinking on the job."

"It's never effected my work, I just need one to stop the shaking," he said.

He was from a dead generation. The man was hard and anything but green. A little rough around the edges but I liked him. He wasn't the typical Boy Scout that wanted the position. "If you'll excuse me for just a moment," I said. The man nodded and I walked out pressing a button as I exited that lifted a wall panel revealing one-way mirror glass. This allowed him to see the room next door. He watched as I walked into a similar adjacent room with an identical chair, except this chair had a man tied to it.

I had become bored with interrogation almost two decades ago. Nothing changed and it's always the same results. Breaking a man was easy and I used to take pride in how fast I could do it but now it became routine. A day job that you had already figured out and were craving something new, but there were always protocols. What made me so good was the research I did into each of my employees to find out what would break them.

"James, how have you been? I heard we had a little mishap in sector seven's lower quarter," I said. "They were aided by a professional. His EMP shock was military grade and knocked out our systems completely, " the man said.

"So you allowed Gothamsreckoning to escape?" I said cutting him off. My head began to throb a bit. *She escaped your so-called genius plan. She'll bite you, you know... She'll bite you just like that bitch did when you were little. It's always a cry for help with you. Weakness coursing through your veins. You think hiring someone else will change that? Have some self-respect and end your miserable existence.* I shook my head wildly slamming my fist against the table. "One year of surveillance, three units working around the clock, the location of her main headquarters with full support and a confirmation of the target's exact location," I said.

The man began to grovel, his voice shaking and desperate, his contagious weakness poisoning the room. "Sir, we can acquire the target again."

"Did you at least identify the unknown?" I asked.

"V...voice recognition came back negative, there wasn't enough time to get a visual before the EMP burst. He had to have been military sir. He reacted to one of the officers engaging his armor piercing rounds prematurely. I tried to ping him but he must have been Special Ops... before the chip implants. No finger prints, no DNA matches, no bullets fired, the man was a ghost. Give me one more chance sir. I promise I won't let you down," he said while his eyes began to tear up a bit.

"Normally in this situation I would slit your throat and watch your life pour out before you but my Brioni suit might get soiled."

"I couldn't do anything sir... I recovered the best I could...I just..." he said.

"There, there..." I said sliding in behind him, blowing my cigars smoke over his shoulder like a dragon. It stung his already tearing eyes. "I know it wasn't your fault and you've done well over the last year." I grabbed a loose rope that dangled above his neck and pulled it hard around his throat. His legs and arms shook furiously as saliva danced in the back of his throat. "I won't accept failure when all the cards are stacked in your favor. I'll send a sweet letter to your wife and kids saying you served bravely in your line of duty." His eyes shot open, probably grasping onto the last image he could conjure of their faces, but at that precious moment I fish hooked them with my middle and pointer fingers. They gave way to the force easy enough, squirting white mucus like fluid onto the desk in front of us as my fingers forced their way deeper into the concave of his eye sockets, encouraged by his screams. His precious memories were erased by the piercing pain he now felt.

I loved taking that moment from people. That one last moment for them to give their final goodbyes and to remember what was truly precious to them before death. It could be taken by simply applying the right amount of pain. Before he could recover from the piercing pain, I snapped his neck.

After wiping my hands off on my handkerchief, I picked up the case file and walked coolly back to the other room where Mr. Miller was now standing in disbelief. His eyes quivered as they traced my steps to the opposite side of the table. I slipped into my chair in a calm manner and asked, "Just wanted to make sure, you did tell me earlier that you wouldn't let me down correct?" The man nodded slowly and uncomfortably. "Good... That's good. You start tomorrow. Here is a case file on Gothamsreckoning. Study it and be ready for your next assignment." I shook his hand and exited the room.

Chapter 21: Rise Up
Source: Encrypted Message
Name: Silvia aka Gothamsreckoning

Sent to the greatest gamers across the globe:

I go by the notorious call sign of Gothamsreckoning. Some of you I have shed blood with, conquered with, and even perished with. Others I have not met but I promise that I have followed you since the moment you opened your eyes into this virtual haven.

I have contacted you because you are the elite, the true spirits, the blood that flows through the veins of VEG, breathing life into its reality. Although ghosts to the real world, I have seen you, truly seen your souls.

I call on you now to rise up in arms against the corporate army that now controls our virtual realm; against the ones that have taken the purity of our existence and turned us upon each other without our consent; against those that have segregated us once again through their capitalistic greed.

The plagues that tore apart the genuine bonds of humanity have transcended the virtual barriers and are now poisoning both worlds. The dream has collapsed upon itself and all of us let it happen, focusing on our own personal gain. I know, because isolation is easier. We see less pain in its existence because we have a close-knit group of users to fall back on. Why care about others when your guild can provide you the support you seek?

I'll tell you why, because we are all one people. VEG was a chance to prove that again, a way to escape the pettiness of our existence and rise to the planes of gods. Once more we are at a cross roads, and once more we are walking through that dark valley where the puppet masters control the upper ground. We cannot see them but we can feel their grip, hiding in the space between the visible code.

That dream of the golden days still exists. Rise now, rise as one with me. I will make that dream a reality. Corporate media would have you believe that I'm a parasite with the sole purpose of destroying VEG. I ask you to open your eyes and break free of the chains that bind you to their system.

Fight with me my brothers and sisters. Fight to take back the spirit of VEG that's slowly dying. Fight the tyranny that has laid waste to both worlds. The final World War is upon us, and we can let it take us over individually or we can join forces and conquer the puppeteers together once and for all.

Fog poured through the skyscrapers of New York City, hugging their frames tight as a lover. The building's lights disappeared into nothingness, lost in heavy dew. It was a dismal setting that ate away at hope and valor, leaving a sour taste in the mouth. For some though, it was home. I reflected on how it reminded me of the end of days, the world after the apocalyptic war that I thought inevitable if tonight's events went south.

Mark stood inches from my side and I could feel his warmth soothing my skin, making my goose bumps subside. I couldn't tell if it was the heat or the intense focus in his manner but something in him made me feel calm and collected as if nothing could go wrong. He had his left arm extended outwards gripping Bell's hand.

I was surprised at how much Bell had taken to her savior. She reacted to him like she would a father figure, tugging on him throughout the car ride, desperately needing his attention in any activity she pursued. Mark reacted well to the initial news of my true identity. Shocked initially, but understanding once I filled him in on the corruption within a sect of our own government.

Evo felt distant, looking into the horizon like there was something no one could see except for him; something looming, weighing on his actions. We all stood on the brim of Central Park, awaiting the army of VEGERS. They trickled in at first amassing like rain droplets into pools of water and soon began pouring out of alleyways and streets like a river.

The horde of system administrators were set up in the Great Lawn of Central Park. They had created an overlay for the entire area to look similar to the Zerg's planet from Starcraft. Starcraft was a real time strategy based game where one was given the choice of three different races to battle each other on distant worlds. Terrans reflected the human race in the future, Protoss were an alien race with advanced technology and warp capability, and Zerg were primal aliens with a hive insect like existence.

The arena that the administrators had chosen looked as if cockroaches had evolved, laying waste to all resources, leaving a barren landscape in their wake. It had the ominous feel of a feeding ground that was moments away from erupting with millions of heartless insects. Patrols of Zerglings and Hydralisks were sporadically stationed throughout its entirety.

Zerglings were alien attack dogs with two extra mammoth scythe-like arms rising from their backs, meant to maim their target. They were highly aggressive, with raptor like speeds. The Hydralisk's base was that of a snakes rising up to a wide elongated alien head. They also had two scythe-like arms as well but their main attack was shooting venom from their mouths, doing damage over time that eroded your armor. There was no simple way through, and just looking at it made you quiver with the sensation of failure before the fight.

Chapter 23: Battle Plan
Source: Journal
Name: Mark Boggs

A man in full samurai armor sat near the entrance to the southern gate with an intricate Katana sword strapped to his back. It had blood smeared and stained on the folded steel as if fresh from battle.

"Kenshin," Evo called out to him as our trio approached.

Kenshin turned and stared as if he were a visage. "Evo?" he said in a dazed state.

"Kenshin old friend, I was hoping you would show," Evo said.

Kenshin came back into focus, "Where are the other inseparable three, you all disappeared for five years?" Kenshin asked with a concerned tone.

Evo brushed the question aside like it hadn't even left his lips. "This is Mark and Gothamsreckoning," Evo said.

Kenshin decided to not press the question, "Gothamsreckoning, the one that called me here. The call to rise up against the administrators. Outgunned but not outnumbered. I like these odds," Kenshin said smiling.

"It's a pleasure to meet you. I've been following your records now for quite some time," Silvia said shaking his hand.

"The pleasure is all mine, I never thought I would stand in the presence of the great and illusive Gothamsreckoning.

My record pales in comparison," Kenshin said doing a formal bow. "I'd have to say that I'm ashamed for thinking that you were a man," Kenshin said as he rose back up to his full and upright position. Silvia's cheeks blossomed with a bashful red.

Kenshin was truly an artist when it came to social situations, "let's get down to business, shall we?" Kenshin pulled up a virtual map of Central Park. He began tapping away at it, manifesting all the known danger areas with Hydralisk and Zergling mobs. Then he continued, "I would try and show you my intricate plan to infiltrate their base but I'm sure it would look like child's play compared to the masterpiece that you've surely orchestrated."

Silvia stepped up without hesitation, taking on a new air of confidence that no one expected. VEG users crammed in around the four of them filling in every void until everyone's body was supported by someone else's. There was a pause, people sat motionless for a bit observing the phenomenon of feeling as one.

Silvia enlarged the virtual map, pointing to the clearing in front of the administrator's fortress. "This is where their main bulk of summons will be, expect to see it all. Every summon you have read about, they will most likely possess and since they control the program, they will have ones you have never seen. Imagine that your strongest summons, spells, and weapons are their weakest."

People shifted uneasily in the crowd of professional veterans. Silvia looked up feeling the hesitation of the unit, "It's ok, I've fought them before. In their arrogance they get sloppy. This match is a joke to them, and they expect to win by a landslide. They will want to test all of their nifty new Frankenstein creations, so they will toy with us like mice.

In that aspect we will have the advantage. Their impatience along with misdirection will be our key to victory." She pointed at a spot on the map. "Once they begin casting here we will flee as a unit. We will lure each summon into traps that will be placed here." She zoomed in on another area of the park a good distance away from the system administrator's fortress.

"At first they won't come, but give it time. I chose you all because you are the best gamers and grinders that VEG has ever seen. The system administrators will become impatient easily. They will send their summons into a zone that we will have covered with mines and traps. Expect two to three summons though. When they pursue, they will most likely not be careless. Once we kill the summons, we will split our army in two. A group of you will head east as fast as you possibly can and the others will sprint northwest at their base again but arriving from a different route. The northwest group will do the whole bait and kill again but change locations of their traps. The group on the east will circle around the outskirts of the park. The administrators will hopefully think that their summons killed off half the army, which will make them cast weaker spells to savor and prolong their war games. Once the second group of summons is killed I want you to sprint back to the base but this time fight. Cast your weakest summons you have. Pull out your low level ranged weapons. The administrators will see how pathetic we are and it will lure them out of the safety of their fortress. This is when I want you to unleash every monthly or annual cool down spell you've ever acquired. Show them why you've been listed as the top ranked VEG players. Show them that with every advantage stacked in their favor that they are weak." The crowd cheered loud and long hooting and hollering like zoo animals crying out for freedom.

Silvia raised her hands up to calm their excitement. "While this all is going on, I want the eastern group to sneak around their entire fortress and attack them from the rear. There is a reinforced door here that can be broken with this weapon." She placed an enormous Dwarvin warhammer on the table with a large spike protruding from its head.

"This is an item that they don't know exists," Silvia smiled looking around at the silenced crowd staring at the hammer's intricate metal work. The head was inlayed with a futuristic timer in its central mass. "Slam this into the door, spike first, and it will activate the bomb inside. Once the timer on its face hits zero it will destroy any door ever created in VEG, killing everyone in its path within line of sight of the door. Storm the castle and go in for close combat kills. This is where our numbers will count and work in our favor. Get in and fight two to three on one. Focus fire on spell casters. At close range they won't have time to conjure summons. Attack fast and with fury. If everything goes right we will walk away with victory."

The crowd was now bouncing with excitement. Silvia placed the warhammer with a user named W@RCHILD. He was a skilled warrior that wielded an overlarge battle-axe, dressed in furs from head to toe, resembling a Viking lord. "W@RCHILD will lead the east army. Protect him at all costs. The warhammer must make it to the back of the fortress."

Silvia began parting the army into east and west, picking them by hand. It was like she had been planning these teams for years. She walked down the line telling each player what to focus on and which combination of items would work best in the situation. A true leader was in their presence and I looked at her now, not as a lover but as a

Genghis, a Caesar, or an Alexander. One could feel the greatness from her touch.

It was funny how you couldn't see a person like that in our current world. Earth didn't have time for heroes, leaders, and conquerors. Our great leaders were probably working on rig platforms as safety leads, teaching kids baseball while working as gas station attendants at night. The great battles had already been fought and won and leaders and warriors alike were now rotting away in their working class slumber, lost in the wrong time period.

Silvia spoke loudly disrupting my tangent, "finally I will have a small group with me and Mark for protection. This will be Kenshin, Evo, and Drogo." Drogo was a speed knight. He was said to be the second best in the nation. "We will be a rogue group that will determine our plan of attack on the fly. If no one has any questions then I wish you all good luck and happy hunting." The crowd formed ranks and began entering Central Park, confident and ready for battle.

Chapter 24: I'm Ready
Source: Journal
Name: Mark Boggs

Silvia placed a pair of Jackers on my head. They felt like an old friend. I never thought I would see the day that I missed the feeling of them resting upon my face. "I hacked your account and gave you a max level warrior with the strongest armor I have acquired over the years," Silvia said while rubbing her hand down the center of my chest.

I pushed the red button on my rod, flames shot out around my body and in an instant I was covered with a molten red lava plate mail. It dripped off my arms and feet igniting the ground with fire every step I took. My right arm transformed into an enormous cannon resembling Mega Man from the old Nintendo game. "Any melee based strikes will deal fifty percent damage back to the attacker. When using your arm cannon just point and shoot. It has a heat seeking function that can't miss. Follow me close and I'll protect you," she said smiling and then pressed her own rod.

Slick oily black armor with streaks of pearl whites rose up her body twirling around her breasts in a Princess Leia fashion. Her character wielded a battle wand, a long metallic staff with sapphires on both ends, which she slammed into the earth.

My lips were upon hers before I had the chance to resist my body's primal urge. She didn't pull back, her body laid into mine, melting into my arms. When I was finally able to pull away, she smiled up at me, "Looks like someone likes my armor."

A barrage of embarrassment flooded my senses. "I'm sorry I..."

Silvia cut me off by placing her hand back on my chest, "its ok... Thank you. I needed that." My arms loosened and released her from my grip letting her stand on her own again.

The army was preparing and Silvia was on her way back to talk with Bell,"I want you to stay here with these two men. They are going to take you to a safe place and watch over you." She nodded to two enormous muscle men, and they took Bell by the arms and began to walk away.

I had been so caught up in the moment that I had completely forgotten about Sally. She hung behind my back leg, hanging on it for protection. "Silvia," I called out. "Could Sally go with them?" Bell turned around with her hand out open palmed before Silvia could even react, saying, "Sally this way."

I bent down and kissed Sally on the cheek. "Daddy, you are going to war?" she asked in a sweet voice.

"Fake war, and Silvia gave me this armor to protect me. It will keep your daddy safe. Go with Bell and I will see you as soon as all this is over." She kissed me and then her little legs carried her over to grip Bell's open hand. I turned away so that I wouldn't have to see her leave.

Silvia rubbed my shoulder gently and said, "She'll be safe with them. I promise." I forced out a smile to appease her. Focusing on the war at hand calmed my nerves. "You ready," Silvia said. I nodded and walked to the entrance of the park.

Chapter 25: The War
Source: Journal
Name: Mark Boggs

The park lay eerily silent, building up unsettling and unshakeable fears. Those thoughts that started innocent but turned evil were now ripping through the minds of the brave. The VEGERS walked as one unit, marching in perfect formation. We had made it a good two miles with little incident. Then without warning the landscape gave way to chaos.

Hundreds of Zerglings came screaming out of the woods from the north, rabid with adrenaline. The chatter of their razor sharp teeth conducting a symphony of panic as they bounded toward the head of the army with cheetah like speeds. In Starcraft the Zerglings were the smallest creatures in the game. Seeing them in VEG was horrifying. They were the size of buffalo and their stampede made everyone's leg sensors tremble with the quaking of the earth.

Silvia slammed her staff into the ground, gripping one of the enormous sapphires on top. It started glowing bright blue and a wall of ice encircled the group. The barrier was forty feet high and fifteen feet thick. "Ranged classes, rain down DPS," Silvia commanded. The group was already in the process, casting meteor strikes and acid rain onto the atrocities as they approached.

The Zerglings slammed into the wall with such force that the first twenty knocked themselves unconscious, sending a rippling crack through its core. The rest encircled the ice leaping at it, desperately trying to break through to feed upon flesh. One of the Zerglings barked out strange noises as it studied the barrier. They began to dig their razor like claws into the ice, climbing it with ease. They were dying but not quick enough.

A Shadow Elf cast a mirror image of himself on the other side of the wall that took on half of his capabilities, trying to draw a chunk of them off. He attacked at their backsides distracting a pack from attempting the climb.

The pack grew in size, chasing the Shadow Elf off to the west. This made the Zerglings coming over the wall easier to handle. Hunters stepped up into positions casting net snares, entangling the beasts that reached the crest. It sent them colliding into the monsters below, twisting limbs to breaking point, crippling a majority of them.

Fire mages burned portal sized windows through the ice so that line of sight attacks were possible and within a few minutes we had killed off the entirety of the horde. Seeing how long it took to kill them was a little intimidating for most but we were still fresh with confidence from the win.

Two more waves of Zerglings attacked on the way to the fortress but only two users perished in the fight. The hives of Hydralisks hadn't appeared in the predicted hostile zones. It had Silvia visibly nervous but she was trying to appear strong for the rest of the users by barking orders. We were approaching the administrator's stronghold and the group slowed in awe of its magnitude.

The fortress was a labyrinth of jagged steel. Guard towers jutted up in every direction with spikes perched precariously about. Two ominous double set doors lurked from its center depicting the gates of hell, with damned souls reaching up to the heavens in desperation, hoping for salvation. A wooden crate lay twenty feet in front of the entrance, tied with a red ribbon, like a present waiting to be opened.

A sole mage appeared in one of the central guard towers holding his wooden staff above his head. He chanted a foul sounding language and the crate's ribbon began to dance around, untying itself. The top of the crate shot into the air and the four walls dropped revealing a baby carriage.

Nothing was visible, but infant squeals rang out from within. They filled the air, turning exponentially darker with each passing second. Then they suddenly stopped. A soft chubby arm reached out gripping the side of the carriage struggling to pull the rest of its body upright. A baby's face popped up, appearing normal at first. Then you saw it; there were no eyes, just black hole like empty sockets. It made my skin crawl the way it looked out upon us, as if it could see into our souls.

The baby lunged from the carriage with super human strength landing in a crouched position, head starring at us cocked to an awkward angle like a zombie. Its chest sucked in and then shot back outwards releasing a lion like roar from deep within.

The baby's body began to shake like it was having a seizure but still, it kept its soulless sockets locked upon us. The skin on the baby's back began rising as the convulsing quickened to a shudder. It expanded rapidly until it exploded, shooting a green puss in every direction, and a horned demon launched out into the air. Its body was shielded in black and red scales, but the beast's stomach was unusual. The belly was made with a transparent skin, resembling glass, so that you could see through to the scales upon its back. No organs were visible, just liquid.

The demon grew a hundred feet within seconds, letting out screeching noises with the shock of its growing pains. The baby's shakes subsided and then it stood upright with its hands extended in the air moving its fingers as if it wanted to be held. The demon's massive head lunged forward, swallowing the baby whole.

Inside the demon's transparent stomach, the baby appeared swimming around until it positioned itself to look back out upon the army of VEGERS. It was suspended, floating in the fluid. The baby lifted its right arm and the demon mimicked the move. It looked as though the baby was the puppet master getting used to the new controls of its toy.

The demon approached, being operated by the abomination within. It lunged at the solid formation of VEGERS grabbing the first user it saw, ripping off his head with his razor sharp teeth. Blood spewed out from the void. It squeezed his body to increase the flow, bathing itself in the glory of the kill. "Run," Silvia screamed. They took off at a sprint but not before the demon slammed his hand down upon two more users, crushing them to death. Hunters tried to cast snares to slow it down but luckily it stopped at the edge of the tree line.

We arrived at the second clearing and formed back into ranks. Silvia called out commands but in mid-sentence a user screamed from the rear of the group. Everyone turned, only to see a hive of Hydralisks striking from the tree line.

There were too many to count and they were slashing and spitting venom with deadly precision. The venom blinded sight and eroded armor. Silvia froze the front line of aggressors in place with her staff but it wouldn't hold for long. "Hunters snare their mouths to stop the venom attack.

Healers cast protective bubbles for the melee, and warriors get to the rear to take the damage," Silvia called out.

The users worked together smoothly to Silvia's surprise. Nature Mages awoke the trees behind them, and they were now slamming down upon the horde of Hydralisks stunning them almost to death. Before long they had the situation under control but they had still lost some of their healers before they could counter the surprise attack. Everyone's armor had been eroded but it was only their secondary armor used to deceive the system administrators into thinking they were weaker.

The trees began to part from the north being pushed aside with ease by the demon and one other large summon that couldn't be made out yet. *Good they only sent two*, Silvia thought. "I need six powerful summons now," Silvia said.

A spirit mage dressed in blue robes and a white skin tight suit pressed a button on her rod changing it into a sacrificial dagger. Raising the blade above her head, she began to speak Spanish in a demonic manner, rocking her body back and forth. She was speaking of death and the day the dead would rise and overtake the earth. Her hands slammed the dagger into her own belly pulling it across horizontally to gut herself. Blood flowed from the opening like a waterfall, cascading over the torn flesh.

The Spirit Mage's eyes turned bright red burning like embers, her chanting turned into a stream of words that were incomprehensible. The pool of her life bulged and when the Spirit Mage's words turned into a scream, the blood blossomed outwards birthing a fifty-foot blood genie. Its body comprised only of thick red blood. It swirled around the base of his body like a hurricane.

The blood genie engulfed the Spirit Mage and they became one. Invoking yourself into a summon was a risky move because when your summon died you perished with it. Although, it was the only way to have a truly powerful summon.

Next an Ice Mage froze the ground in front of himself, placing a bright blue stone in the center. It sparkled like the universe. Shooting stars, galaxies, and cosmos radiated from within. A Fire Mage lit the ball on fire, which sent the universe into chaos. The Ice Mage quickly froze it in a cocoon of ice.

At its core, something white was twirling inside. An animal was taking form and growing exponentially. A polar bear broke free of its frozen barrier sending shards of crystal ice flying into the air. It grew ten times the size of an elephant. When standing upright, it was as tall as the administrators demon summon. He roared, bearing his pearly white teeth, batting at the skies with his massive paws.

Two hunters, who had been conversing early in the game, both launched Mega Mole summons. They placed a peanut shaped rock on the ground and had a Dwarf smash them with a warhammer. The earth split and shook, until two moles came digging upwards revealing only the top halves of their gargantuan bodies. It was a great idea to cast Mega Moles, because they could hold summons in place rooting them to the ground while attacking.

Finally a Fire Mage whispered some words to his wooden staff to ignite it with flames. Fire spread from the staff, engulfing his entire body, until he was glowing bright red. Pointing his staff at the sky, every bit of the inferno launched from him shooting straight into the overcast sky.

A halo of fire spread through the clouds from the beam, opening a portal in which a fire breathing red dragon came soaring through.

The dragon swooped down and landed next to the Fire Mage nuzzling his head while smoke poured through his nostrils, drenching him in it. The Mage rubbed his nose and touched his wand to his forehead. In an instant the dragon was covered in steel armor from head to toe with two large proton cannons strapped to his sides. Hunters were carefully lacing the tree line with giant traps and Dwarves were busy setting bombs underground to greet the administrator's summons. Then we waited.

The initial attack was chaos. Silvia had figured that only two summons would approach from the front but another two surprised us from the rear. The traps that were laid crippled the first summon to come bursting through the trees. What was once an axe wielding Minotaur, was now a legless desperate animal wailing for mercy. He received that mercy from the polar bear summon, that swallowed his head whole, spitting out his horns with a fierce look of disgust.

It was a short-lived victory that ended with the two summons attacking from the rear. The red dragon was yanked out of the sky by a zombie werewolf that lunged at it from a treetop and one of the Mega Moles was plucked from the ground like a vegetable by the power of the demon summon. It tossed the mole about like a rag doll. He threw it to a Titan that ripped it limb by limb juggling its body parts as a jester would.

The polar bear was defending desperately against the demon. The werewolf and the Titan had set upon the blood genie and the mole. When the Titan opened his mouth to bite off the second mole's head the blood Genie morphed into liquid and leapt into his throat. The titan began to glow red, shaking and convulsing. Rocks shed from his exterior until the red overtook him. All of the sudden the Titan stood up straight as if it was a new entity. The blood Genie had taken control.

The Titan rounded on his heels and grabbed the werewolf by the throat. In one quick motion he ripped out its esophagus and watched him bleed out as he roared with laughter. The demon was still aggressing and had now met up with the Titan. The other summons were hardly a match. "Split," Silvia screamed over the panic filled battlefield. They did so but not before losing another twenty-two users.

The plans had to adapt because of the losses in the first wave. She texted new orders to the west army, but kept the original plan for the group now fleeing to the east. The administrator's summons engaged the western army to Silvia's relief, but the texts pouring in on their visors told of an awful ambush that awaited them at the second rendezvous point.

The western army was destroyed and it hadn't even been two hours into the war. Silvia stopped in a panic holding her chest as she collapsed. She began rubbing it, gasping for air. Her hand stopped in place with a sudden realization and then she was back on her feet sprinting in an unknown direction. Kenshin, Evo, Drogo, and I were on her six, our legs coursing with exhaustion to try and keep her pace. The route was long and obscure to evade detection but the end point was that of question.

We stood in front of the Charles Sanders statue, erected in the northern part of Central Park. It was a clearing that left us exposed. We stood one hundred yards from the eastern wall of the administrator's fortress. They were already screaming commands at each other from the watchtowers. "Silvia we can't hold this position. What are we doing here?" Kenshin asked. "I need 5 minutes," Silvia said.

Hordes of enemy users were pouring in around us. "What in the fuck is she doing, this is suicide." Drogo said as he sprinted toward the raiding horde. Silvia worked in a methodical and efficient fashion. She pressed the front of Charles Sanders belt buckle, while stepping on his right foot, then reached up and pulled his eyelids closed.

The key from around Charles's neck popped out of the statue and into her hand. She unzipped her black leather jacket, revealing a golden necklace with a key at the end. With a quick yank it came free, breaking the golden chain that held it. With a couple of movements she had locked the keys together. "We don't have much time," Kenshin yelled, glimpsing back.

"One more minute," Silvia yelled, as she placed the key inside the globe shaped chest. It made a hissing noise and then physically opened. An augmented ball of energy came rising out of its center, suspended in midair. She grabbed the ball and placed it on the ground in front of us speaking words in Latin that I couldn't make out. The ground began to rumble, the rumble turned to quake, and the quake split the earth in four directions opening to its core.

The army of enemy users all came to a standstill watching in awe. Even Kenshin had stopped fighting the entirety of administrators and turned facing toward the point that Silvia was crouched over. An eruption of lava came rocketing upwards from the crumbling earth, sending flaming fireballs in every direction. One of the fireballs landed on a VEG administrator, mesmerized with wonder of the summoning spectacle. It killed him instantly.

His death sent the administrators into a panic. They began running in every direction to evade the eruption's fury. When the smoke cleared and only ash rained down upon Central Park, a long shrieking primal scream echoed from below, and a booming voice called out "ROSHAN AWAKES," that reached every corner of the park.

It had been said that Charles Sanders favorite video game was called Defense of the Ancients or DotA for short. It was a multiplayer battle arena mod made from the strategy game Warcraft III, an older type of League of Legends game. Roshan was a boss that players could join together to kill, giving their team an advantage of levels, gold, one free life, and a piece of cheese that replenished mana and health.

From the depths of the quake's core rose an enormous rock hand, digging its fingers into the edge of the ground. Roshan, in full armor, pulled himself upwards as if born from the depths of hell, lava pouring off his plate mail.

When visible, Roshan was mesmerizing to look at, a monstrosity whose body was comprised of boulder like stones, now towering over everything in the park. He stood the size of the Empire State Building, the tanks and summons that plagued the field were that of ants in comparison. She directed it upon the enemy horde.

She wiped out half of their castle with a single swing of his arm. The summon was just a myth that had been talked about on game forums and blogs. No one believed in its existence.

The entire field stopped in motion, frozen as a computer would during an MMO when the server was overloaded. Silvia appeared to be in her element, crushing and bashing atom sized enemy users. She approached the last standing barricade of the castle with the remaining administrators inside. They didn't try and run or hide. A sole unarmed dead Warrior walked toward her. Others began to follow. Even dead users began walking behind the Warrior, disobeying the PvP rules. The Warrior came to a stop in front of Silvia. The entire army had filed in behind him. Administrators and allies alike were standing at attention.

The Warrior did a slight bow and then knelt down on one knee. He placed his right hand over his chest and lowered his head. In unison the rest of the users did the same. There was silence across the entire park. Hundreds of users were bent over doing what appeared to be the accolade ceremony. Tears began to run down Silvia's cheeks. She approached the Warrior and touched the back of his head. I stood motionless not knowing what was happening or what everyone understood. Whether enemy or ally they looked as though they were swearing loyalty, as if they knew some silent secret that I didn't.

My visor filled up with a large "VICTORY" in double bold font. The other team had forfeited, and over eighty percent had been banned for a month. It was over, and the field was engulfed in cheers. Silvia dismissed Roshan and grabbed Evo and I's hands saying, "it's time."

The VEG Headquarters was an easy breach. Silvia had done her fair share of breaking and entering over the years. We entered through the back as to go undetected. Once inside, Silvia linked a live map that displayed the exact location of each security guard in my Jackers.

My feet glided silently across the marble floors, my body finding the rhythm of the hunt. There were no screams, no grunts or cries for help, just muffled struggles that were short lived. I swept through the guards within the hour and the building lay quiet. Once finished, Silvia kicked back into gear, eager to lead the way.

My pointer finger rubbed the side of my Glock 17 like prayer beads hoping for good fortune as Silvia, Evo, and I ran through the maze of hallways in the VEG headquarters. Silvia darted left and right down unmarked corridors with an eerie familiarity as if running through her old neighborhood. I had stopped questioning her copious amounts of secret knowledge.

We arrived at a steel door with an advanced security system. She pressed her palm against a reader to her right. Lasers shot out, scanning her retina and then prompted her for a voice recognition pass code. "Silvia," she said. Evo was pacing back and forth behind me.

"Identity confirmed. Welcome Silvia," a robotic voice said. The metallic door groaned and slid upwards.

The room was dark to the degree that shadows died in its depths. Silvia fumbled around for some kind of switch on the wall when the metal door came slamming down behind us, cutting off our only exit.

"Silvia Sanders," said a voice darker than the room itself. It lurked from an unknown origin. I pointed my Glock into the void abyss. Then the name registered in my brain. *Sanders.... Sanders, Charles Sanders. It all makes sense. The daughter of Charles Sanders...* before I could process further, I felt the cold nozzle of a gun press firmly against my temple.

"Drop it," said a voice that was rougher than the first. His breath reeked of cheap cigarettes, whiskey, and experience. A soft click, and the entire scene illuminated.

"The daughter of the creator himself," said a scarecrow of a man. The skin on his face looked as though it was shrink wrapped to his skull, accenting his hollow cheeks. He looked malnourished, evil in nature, as though he fed on souls of the weak.

Black eyes peered around the room, gazing in amusement. Dark shades lined his lids that only an insomniac portrayed. His crisp black suit looked to empower his esteem. "I had tried to have all of Charles's access denied upon his death, but alas, the man surprises me from the afterlife. I didn't think you had survived our successful attempt on your mother, but I stand corrected." Silvia shivered like a puppy during a lightning storm.

"Oh pardon my manners. Introductions are always the proper way to begin. My name is... well you can call me Mr. Smith. My esteemed colleague over here, that as far as I can tell has already become properly acquainted, is Mr. Miller."

He made a throat clearing sound and locked his eyes upon me.

The room froze in place, quiet to the point of discomfort. "Who are you?" I managed to force out, feeling the gun on my temple shift with the movement of my jaw.

Mr. Smith looked as though he had become annoyed. "As to not sound redundant, and to educate you on the formalities of introduction, I will do this for you. Your name is Mark Boggs, a retired military Special Forces veteran, who found solace in the bottle after his family was torn apart by one life altering event. A man who quite ironically tore apart my plans of ending Gothamsreckoning's life in her main headquarters."

Silvia glanced at me before turning back to Mr. Smith. He had us all at attention like we were grade school children being lectured by the principal.

"How did you..." "How did I know your identity? Let's just say I pride myself on being resourceful," Mr. Smith said, cutting my words short.

He turned his predatory gaze upon Silvia. "The prodigious daughter survives." He clapped his hands slow and rhythmic before continuing, "the thorn in my sweet rose, but what came as a curse could turn to a cure if we are all forthcoming. Your father, after we turned him into a paranoid delusional, decided to place certain... restrictions upon our access to VEG. One of which, but of course not all, is the lock that keeps us from having full control. The other is his portion of the profits. He found a way to keep a percentage of his shares of VEG flowing to his home in the afterlife. I can only assume that Daddy's funds have been spent well upon this little uprising of yours."

Mr. Smith placed a revolver on the table in front of him. Servers flashed red behind him shedding an ominous light upon the silver barrel of the gun. He tapped it lightly with his forefinger.

"How did you know my location?" Silvia asked, needing to know the answer to the one question that had been lingering in her mind. Mr. Smith jumped upwards slamming both of his palms face down on the table. "Now that, is an excellent question!" he said with a maniacal expression. "Mr. Miller would you be so kind as to show our guests what lies behind door number one?"

Miller was good, he drew away slow, but kept his gun aimed at my temple. He faded out of my peripheral vision and I heard a soft click from my rear. The east wall opened up to reveal three unknown individuals. Two Caucasian males of medium build and one slender Asian female were sitting unconscious and duct taped to chairs. They were malnourished, their figures anorexic in a way that only POW's knew.

Evo drew his weapon in a blurred haste and locked it upon Mr. Smith's forehead. "I'm sure you have impeccable accuracy with that thing Evo, but before you squeeze the trigger allow me to shed a little light on one minor detail. Within this adjacent room is a quite fascinating device. Now this machine in particular, was a product of failure," Mr. Smith said looking around the room as if he were waiting for us to take interest in his lesson. There was a tiny black box in the other room with a nozzle at one end facing the hostages. It looked like a miniature fog machine. The man continued, "Let me explain. During an interrogation, one can only have the upper hand if he has leverage over the prisoner. We found in the past, that unless the threat was foolproof, there was a small chance of failure. This machine is capable of releasing enough Sarin gas to kill a population of one thousand. Overkill I know, but I guess you could say I enjoy being thorough. Now Sarin gas, for those of you that don't know is a lethal nerve agent. After initial exposure, you feel your chest begin to tighten, then the fun part begins. The victim loses control of all their bodily functions dying in a pool of their own vomit, shit, and piss," he said with a theatrical smile.

Mr. Smith removed a keypad from his pocket, it was square in shape and the keys were backlit with neon blue. "This is the keypad that operates our little machine in the adjacent room. Our first prototype of this device had a remote keypad with a simple red button to trigger the release. It was not as sleek and aesthetically pleasing as this one," he said, turning the keypad over in his hand admiring its design. "It was more raw and boxy but it served its purpose all the same. It was placed in the hand of the interrogator, and it had an astonishing ninety nine percent success rate. But in one instance we found the interrogator dead on the floor, his jaw dislocated, with the bulky red buttoned remote lodged in his throat." Mr. Smith pushed nine or ten numbers on the keypad and then continued. "Where was I? Oh yes... you see, failure is a beautiful dilemma, because with failure, something simple becomes complex. The system evolves into something foolproof. My little remote keypad has a code that must be input once every ten minutes or...well you know the rest. My life before this very moment was merely an obstacle, but now I become needed, one of the most valuable assets you have in the room." He said, flashing a sick sadistic smile at us.

Mr. Smith paused longer than normal, this time starring down the barrel of Evo's pistol. "I've never been a firm believer in the underdog. I don't like the notion of chance.

With that being said I'd hate to let our friends expire prematurely."

Evo's central mass waivered a bit and then he turned the weapon upon Silvia.

"Evo?" Silvia said shocked.

"There that's much better," Mr. Smith said, easing his posture as he sank into the intricate web that he was spinning.

Evo's eyes were tearing up. "I'm sorry... I love her. I thought he would only arrest you. He swore to me. He promised that no one would get hurt... there was no other way. He took the only people that I ever cared about... told me he would hurt them... hurt them if I didn't get close to you." Evo was breaking down, his arm struggling to hold the weight of his gun.

"And I won't hurt them now that you..."

Evo snapped back like a viper at Mr. Smith. "You shut up..." He launched across the room in a blur and gripped Mr. Smith by his throat, lifting him a foot off the ground. "Release them... Release Kira for god's sake... Sarin gas? I gave you what you wanted. You never said anything about this. You said they would be safe. Gave me your word that they would be safe." Mr Smith didn't gasp for air; he hardly even struggled as if he couldn't feel his jugular crushing under Evo's strangling grip. His hand reached slowly into his pocket and presented the keypad before Evo's eyes. Evo's fingers uncoiled, retreating from his neck, shaking with torn emotions.

"It was you who sold us out?" Silvia's voice sounded soft and betrayed. Then it turned harsh, "My friends... your friends Evo. Your fucking friends. My daughter. They could have killed my only daughter. How long?" She crossed the room and slapped him hard across the face. "How long have you been his informant? How long have you served the man that killed my mother and father? The man that took everything that was dear to me and ripped it away." She slapped him again. "You were my friend." He was cowering away from her now, but confused he drew his gun back up waving the barrel back and forth between the two.

Silvia stepped away from him, noticing his failing mental state. Evo's left hand was now pounding at his head and ripping at his hair, sanity fading with each passing second. He lifted his head back up and focused his attention in my direction with a crazy look in his eyes. "And you! Why did it have to be you?" he asked a rhetorical question, the familiarity in his voice startled me.

He dug the barrel of the gun back and forth into his forehead, scraping at his hairline like some kind of rabid animal. "I'm sorry, I'm so sorry," he said as he dropped to his knees sobbing. Rocking back and forth, he held his gun like he was deep in prayer.

The circus act of Evo had everyone's attention except for Mr. Miller's. His gaze rested upon the sight finder of his pistol that was locked upon me with a cold calculation. The man was a soldier, and he was hawk eyeing my every movement, the twitch under my right eye, the stiffness of my fingers, even the particles that cycled through my respiratory system. He could see it all and I felt frozen with fear for the first time since my service. Evo's words had become a jumbled mess and I tried to nod in an understanding manner to comfort him, seeing that I was the current subject of his psycho babblings. The man had no honor and his words fell short.

My mind was focused on an unexpected pawn move that would go unseen to set them up for checkmate. I couldn't think. Mr. Miller's gun and gaze had a grip on me and I could feel my heart thumping inside my chest. Sweat leapt from my hair like rain, sliding down to my lips, filling them with a salty taste.

"...Sally," I snapped back to attention when I heard Evo say my daughter's name.

"What?" I asked but my question turned everyone silent.

Silvia was staring at Evo in disbelief. Evo looked up at me in horror and then went back to his rocking.

"I think I might be able to shed light on the situation. Do you believe in fate Mr. Boggs?" Mr. Smith said but I had lost sight of the conversation.

"What?"

"Fate, Mr. Boggs. It's a simple concept. The idea that our lives are predetermined and that we get what we deserve. I myself have never been a firm believer in the idea but our current situation has me doubting."

Mr. Smith leaned forward in his chair and crossed his hands. "I'd like to tell you a story. Stop me if you've heard it. A man serves his country, seeing and doing things that no man should ever have to do in order to protect certain freedoms that we take for granted. He comes home to find solace in his wife but can't kick his night terrors that haunt his every action. They have a child, a surprise that at first overwhelms but then bears fruit that heals the man's troubled past. His precious little drop of sunshine buys him a game called VEG, which is ironic for a reason that I will get to later."

Silvia was now staring at me. I felt my mind turning to Sally, alone in some unknown location. "Another man unknown to the first starts his life as a failure, an overweight outcast to society. He finds purpose in a game that allows him to shed the extra pounds and become an elite ranked user and respected individual. By some act of luck he manages to catch the fancy of a beautiful woman. They fall in love and live out the whole fairytale of the perfect relationship." Mr. Smith seemed amused with his own words.

I hated the man and wanted him to shut up but his story was gnawing at something inside me. He continued to my dismay, "the man in love gets in a car one beautiful morning. I'm sure the sun was shining and the birds were chirping and love songs were lingering in the air. His mind was so distracted with this new found relationship that he hardly noticed the little bump on a quaint residential street."

Something tugged soft on my sleeve. I looked down and saw Sally's two round beautiful blue eyes staring up at me. They were concerned and scared. "Daddy, I don't like this man. I want to go home," she said waving my arm back and forth as her head darted around.

"Alright now we will be able to go in a minute," I said to calm her anxiety. I got down to her level and kissed her forehead. She loved it when I did that.

"Stop it," Silvia said. Mr. Smith was now smirking with a ruthless smile. He continued with his voice raised, "The police said it was a horrific scene. A little girl with a backpack on was playing unsupervised in the street when she was killed by a hit and run. She died in her father's arms, a decorated war veteran that should've been watching her. This single act brings these two separate realities crashing together without their knowledge."

Sally started coughing and her eyes shot into the back of her head. She was gasping for air. "Sally, SALLYYY... HELP, HELP ME," I couldn't get her to focus. I picked her up into my arms and put my hand to her chest. Her heart was beating so fast. The look in her eyes was pure fear. "SALLY! SALLY!" Blood shot out of her nostrils and poured onto my pants. Her body began to convulse on my lap. "Oh Goddddddd... GODD NOOOOOO. HELP ME." I looked at Silvia and she was motionless. Evo was still shaking back in forth on the ground with his head tilted in shame. "WHAT ARE YOU STANDING AROUND FOR? HELP ME," I screamed.

Mr. Smith was wide eyed now. He began yelling over the top of Sally's gurgles for life, "Let's continue the story Mr. Boggs. The war veteran's daughter is killed by a freak hit and run accident. The police fall short in their investigation, mostly by my doing. They come to the conclusion that an illegally operating VEG player was responsible for the act and had acquired their gear from the notorious Gothamsreckoning!" Sally was turning white as a sheet and I was shaking her trying to make her come to. My hands were dripping with her blood. I began giving her mouth to mouth trying to force air into her little chest between the coughing fits.

"This is where it gets really good! This highly decorated veteran hits the bottle to try and drink away his pain. After his wife leaves him, he joins a collection agency to hunt and arrest illegally operating VEG users, desperately clinging to the hope that one day he would come face to face with the person solely responsible for the death of his daughter. Weeks become months, and months become years without success. This poor grieving father, in a desperate attempt to salvage his sanity, manifests a version of his daughter that he takes on his hunts. It keeps the demons at bay, allowing him to focus on the job at hand, and in turn makes him forget the real reason that he began hunting Gothamsreckoning in the first place.

"Daddy," Sally said her hand resting upon my face. She was younger now, still covered in blood but calm. "Daddy I love you.... I love you always. You are my hero." My tears rushed over her face turning red as they mixed with her blood, crashing to the street below. Red lights flashed invasively in a bombarding blur. The screams of my wife rang out in my ears.

"You can't leave us, I need you baby, I can't live without you," I said trying to squeeze her back to life.

"It's ok Daddy…you will be ok. It's not your fault." Her eyes didn't blink they just stared at me. "I will always be with you Daddy. Let go… Let go…"

It was her hand that faded first, pixels dissolved in front of me, dancing around in circles before disappearing into nothingness. I gripped at it but it was gone before I could touch it. Then her body started to go. I grabbed at it wildly, as the weight of her being seemed to disappear. "SALLY…WAIT. WAIT….NOOO….GODDDD NOOOOO," I screamed. Her blue eyes were still locked onto mine and she was smiling. I couldn't stop crying but she was so calm. Her smile was beautiful; her rosy red plump cheeks were perfect. She was my angel. My little sweet angel with bright blue eyes like her mother. Then she vanished, like the

augmented reality I had become so used to. She was gone....
forever. Then something came over me and I sang.

"Sleep deep and long my children
Without worry of work or time
Keep and cherish innocence
And always be sublime.

Sleep deep and long my children
Sleep past the darkest day
Keep blind to pain and heartache
Sleep troubled times away.

Sleep deep and long my children
Sleep through your regret
Right now sleep for all of us
Have dreams you never forget."

Mr. Smith was bathing in the moment. His skin shivered with delight. "Some people may call me evil, sick, or twisted but I know what I am. By an act of fate, your true enemy stands before you. The man solely responsible for countless years of misery." Mr. Smith rubbed my back. "I can't imagine what you must be feeling right now. I myself have never been a family man but I understand revenge all too well."

Mr. Smith cocked a revolver and placed it in my lap and then walked back to his desk. "I tried to turn myself in," Evo said desperately. *Shut up,* my thoughts screamed but my throat was dry and only hissed when I opened it.

"I sat in my car outside the station calling Kira's phone. It just kept ringing. I wanted to tell her goodbye... tell her how I was sorry, and how much I loved her. It rang and rang and rang... and then my phone rang. I picked it up and a man's voice was on the other end; a man's voice that I never wanted to have sound familiar. A man's voice telling me that my only friends would be killed if I didn't listen to him, didn't do exactly as he said," Evo still wouldn't make eye contact. He was staring at a spot on the floor but his eyes seemed distant.

"He said that Gothamsreckoning had shown interest in me and that I could get close, that I was saving our nation and doing our country a great service." Evo crawled toward me, dragging his hands and feet as if he didn't deserve to have control of them. "I had only seen a picture of you, a picture that he would wave over my head when he felt he was losing his grip on me... I'm sorry. I'm so sorry. It was a fraction of a second," Evo said grabbing the silver muzzle of the revolver and placing it against his forehead, "a fraction of a second that caused an eternity of pain."

I covered his mouth with my hand squishing his face closed until silence gripped him. A fire was rising inside me, the need to destroy existence in its entirety. The overwhelming sensation of self-destruction seized me. I wanted to blow my brains out, I wanted to drink barrels of vodka, I wanted to gut myself and eat my insides; I needed to lose myself...

My mind was in a psychotic frenzy that I couldn't control, like I was jacked up on a mountain of cocaine, zooming through every painful thing I could do to myself. Blood began to ooze out of Evo's lips as I felt his gums give way to his front teeth. "Mark no," Silvia screamed. Her words were void of meaning. They entered my ears only to be devoured by the psychotic storm brewing in my brain. And that gun, that fucking gun watching me...watching my pain from Mr. Miller's hands.

I didn't feel the bullets pass through. I only felt Mr. Miller's face caving under my force. I was upon him in an instant, playing in his brain matter, tossing and turning it in my fists to the screams that filled the room. The bump in my face could have been a bullet but I wasn't sure, the realm where physical pain existed was lost.

Something distant called upon me. The hollow man, demanding control of my chaos, attempting to leverage his gun. A physical toy that bore no threat. It waved in his hand, his words banging louder in my head than the gun's caliper. That sickening boom of his voice drew me away from the soft putty that was once Mr. Miller's head. I charged. I felt a jab to my chest and shoulder, two thumps... it kind of tickled.

The weight of Mr. Smith's body might work. It was light, but manageable. The scarecrow had just enough meat on him to break through the double paned glass that separated us from the adjacent room. "Wait, wait, you need me. You'll all die. This country... No this WORLD NEEDS ME. They'll kill us all you fucking CHINK, YOU CHINK LOVING MOTHER FU..." he screamed but I couldn't understand it. It was all gibberish like a made up language that held no value. I laughed at its alien sound.

The Sarin gas device fit perfectly down his esophagus with the proper amount of force. Blood filled in around it, gurgling in his throat... His cries and screams muffled to his drowning song. I think I remember a story he told about the device and someone's esophagus, or maybe I saw it in a movie. I couldn't remember, I was too busy emptying the contents of a trashcan to think. It had a military grade black bag inside that wrapped nicely around his head. I was happy that he used duct tape on the prisoners because it made it easier to seal the bag to his throat. A front row seat to his death sounded glorious, a one-way ticket to the beyond. Something pulled at my body, yanking me from my prime time view. It dragged me through the door. I struggled to watch, to see the gas consume his body. I wanted to see it spray from all of his orifices. Tentacles of arms restrained my thrashes, and pulled me into darkness. I would only be able to imagine. My eyes grew heavy, weighted by evil dreams. *Goodbye Mr. Smith... Goodbye world.... Goodbye Sylvia... Come now darkness, and swallow me whole...*

Chapter 28: Reboot
Source: Personal Computer Log
User: Evo

My jaw was dislodged but it got knocked back into place by Mark's shoulder during the struggle. It still felt loose and blood oozed through the punctures in my upper lip. Kira came to when I ripped the duct tape from her wrists. She had managed to stop most of the initial bleeding from my mouth, using cloth and tape to fashion a make shift bandage. It held fine until we found a first aid kit in a room down the hall.

Silvia was busy working on Mark. His breathing was shallow and quick and he was covered in blood. Mr. Miller's first shot blew through the side of his cheek and the second grazed his neck. Mr. Smith got a clean shot into his right shoulder, the wound was the one that was spewing the most blood. His eyes were twitching, and his body shook from time to time. I had never seen someone take that kind of beating and continue on.

Silvia worked methodically mending each wound in turn until she had them all cleaned and bandaged. She gave him a large dosage of sedatives to keep him out. He had almost snapped Phantoms throat during the struggle. Phantom still had his hand on his neck, rubbing it back and forth, although he looked just happy to be alive. We left Kira to watch over Mark as we continued on our mission.

Silvia had convinced us there was a second server room that we all hoped wasn't filled with an obscene amount of Sarin gas. We figured that both of the rooms were airtight or else we would have all been dead by now, unless Mark's contraption miraculously held.

It took Silvia awhile but she eventually found a back door entrance. She was able to use her name on every voice recognition panel to get us there. Some of the panels she had to enter codes that she had known by heart. It was like she was back here with her father on a take your daughter to work day.

I could feel the hatred pouring from her. She wanted me dead and her feelings mixed with my own shame. For some reason she wanted me with her. She needed my help. After a couple more turns we came to a door that lead us back to the main server control room. We took a breath and it was clean, I didn't convulse and no one threw up.

In the center of the server room there was a control panel suspended in midair. The problem was that any time we went near it, it turned off. It was like some kind of invisible force field was there that we couldn't see. "This is God, as my father liked to call it... the brain of the entire VEG system. I only ever heard my dad talk about it. This is what I have spent my whole life looking for," Silvia said in a whisper.

"How did they operate it without your father?" Knightcr@wler asked.

"They didn't. My father gave them access to everything else. With access to God though, we can control everything." Silvia walked around the invisible barrier mesmerized by the glowing control panel five feet away.

"I thought you wanted to shut it down?" I said.

"My father told me to never trust anyone completely, he was a smart man. I never intended on destroying it. I'm going to take control, release it to the public, and continue to be the notorious Gothamsreckoning. Except now, I will have full control of VEG and the government will be hunting a ghost. Any profits will go back to the people. VEG was meant for all of us. It was the dream, the dream that would one day transcend to reality. My father could see it and so can I. VEG isn't a game. It's the path back to humanity," she said.

"Look through your Jackers," Silvia said placing her own on her head.

"Look!" Knightcr@wler said. There was a glowing blue block surrounding the control panel. It was pulsing with energy waves and as soon as I slid my hand through it the device's power went dead.

"It's a VEG lock, a magic cube. Give me the sword Evo," Silvia said. Knightcr@wler, Phantom, and I looked at Silvia puzzled. "You think I happened to find you because you were the best of the best? Apparently, while you were deceiving me I was using you. Five years ago you and your friends went on a quest that my father designed; a quest that had been kept safe due to the difficulty of even finding it. You found a sword and that sword is the only item in VEG that can break this lock. I couldn't tell you because I didn't trust you and rightfully so.

"Evo, the sword!" Knightcr@wler said.

"Enders Quest," I whispered taking my rod out. "The sword had ghost stats. Not a single Spell of Identify could tell us a thing about it. We never really got to test it before..." I pressed the red button on my rod and a blue glowing blade manifested itself with an intricate solar systems engraved in its steel. I raised it above my head and slashed it through the center of the force field. Upon contact it exploded into a universe, filling the room. Solar systems radiated overhead. Shooting stars blanketed the skies. The control panel was glowing even brighter now and Silvia walked to it. It was the moment she had been waiting for her entire life. She took a deep breath and grabbed her destiny.

Chapter 29: Forgiveness
Source: Personal Computer Log
User: Evo

My hands trembled upon the car door. The strength in my fingers seemed incapable of performing the simplest task. A laugh manifested itself from somewhere deep in my chest, escaping my sealed lips to reveal itself. It was irony or torture that played in the depths of my uncontrollable laughter. Tears rushed from my eyes, and I felt a moment from breaking down. I took deep breaths in between the laughter and tears to calm myself.

The police station was just outside and I realized that I didn't have a plan for who would take my car once I turned myself in. This was the second time I had done the supposed right thing. This time it didn't feel like the right thing.

Kira had begged me not to go. She said that Mark had forgiven me and that I should forgive myself. He was a better man than I was. I knew it. I felt it. I couldn't forgive myself. I waited five grueling years to hold Kira again; to see my long lost friends. She was more beautiful than I could have possibly remembered. I don't know what happened to them in captivity and I didn't want to know but Kira cried the first couple of nights. I didn't know if it was because of how happy she was to be free with me or because of the things he had done to her. Regardless of the reason, I knew that she needed me more than ever to help her through it.

A moment changed my life, but Mr. Smith gave me the torture of prolonging my judgment, giving the mind time to dwell, giving the heart time to hurt, and giving the soul time to forget. It was the most painful thing I had ever done leaving her love and warm embrace. I killed a man's daughter. I drove off, leaving a little girl named Sally there to die because of my love for Kira. Leaving a daughter dead and a father empty. There was no forgiveness in the world and life never works out the way you think it will. With that, I opened the car door and walked into the police station.

The station was barren. A robotic AI officer with androgynous human traits sat behind a desk with a smile on its face. "Welcome to the New York City police department, how may I help you?" the robot said.

"I'd like to turn myself in for the hit and run resulting in the death of eight year old Sally Boggs," I said.

"Yes sir, please place your hand on the desk so we can verify your identity," the robot said.

A human would have reacted with emotion once I announced that I killed an eight-year-old little girl. Guns would be drawn and I doubted I would be standing. It was a little more civil but right now I wanted the pain to let me know that I was scum. I wanted a knee lodged into my back and a gun pressed against my temple.

I placed my palm on the table and the robot reacted in turn. "Thank you sir. We the state of New York find you not guilty for the death of Sally Boggs."

"What?" I said in a daze.

"Yes sir, the felon responsible for the death of Sally Boggs is New York City resident Samuel Smith, now deceased," the AI officer stated. *Samuel Smith, Mr. Smith?* I thought to myself. Anger flooded my senses.

"That's impossible, I did it!" I yelled slamming my palms on the desk. "Arrest me. Throw me in jail. Lock me away for life." I couldn't shake the guilt from my mind.

"Sorry sir, we have one hundred percent confirmation of suspect, thank you and have a good day," the robot said. Then it disappeared into the floor along with the desk and I was left in an empty room with nothing to scream at or kick.

A message popped up on my VEG Jackers that very instant stating the following:

EVO,

Forgiveness is impossible to accept if we haven't forgiven ourselves. We are bound by the choices we make and I can't begin to imagine what you or Mark have gone through in the last five years. I do know that we all make mistakes. We show character by how we deal with those mistakes. Everyone deserves a second chance no matter what wrong they have committed. Love yourself as I love you and Kira loves you. Go back to your friends and commit to healing them. They need you now as I once did. You are a good man. Live your life. Forgive yourself as Mark and I have forgiven you.

Love,
Silvia.

She had erased my case and framed Mr. Smith. Her control of the world went beyond what I thought imaginable.

A bit of weight felt as though it was lifted from my chest. I felt guilty for feeling excited to go home to Kira but it was only natural after how long we had been apart. My hands were still shaking though. Time, I would just need time. I stepped out in the sunlight. I stepped back out into the world.

Chapter 30: Home
Source: Journal
Name: Mark Boggs

I came to in a comfy bed with flowers in the window, it looked familiar but recalling the memory made my head throb. The room reeked of sterilization. It smelt like a hospital from the fifties. Bell was sitting beside my bed playing with little figurines, while Silvia was sleeping in a chair in the corner. Whatever meds they had me on made my mind feel numb and I was happy for it. Bits and pieces of the prior night flashed back to me, but mostly Sally.

It took me four days to get on my feet. On the second night being bedridden, Silvia and Bell both fell asleep cuddled up next to me. I didn't say much and they didn't seem to expect me to. They had taken me to the cabin in the middle of nowhere to nurse me back to health. Hospitals were out of the question for fugitives, and I liked the seclusion. The dreams were still haunting me but the longer I spent around Bell and Silvia the less the night terrors took me.

Saying goodbye to your daughter is something no man should ever have to do. I've been broken for so long that I couldn't come to terms with the comfort that now filled my life. It made me edgy, like something was waiting around the corner to bite me. A little cabin in the woods is what I managed to end with. A little log cabin filled with a new beginning, laughter, and a woman and child that loved me. It was a feeling that had been long gone and almost forgotten, a family.

The smoke cleared, a daunting dark and narrow staircase beckoned our group below. I was the first to enter, it was reminiscent to Knightcr@wler's basement, and smelt musty. There were pixel graphic art pieces lining the walls, glorifying all of the old classic console games. We descended past Mario, Zelda, Dragon Warrior, Metroid, Final Fantasy, Ninja Gaiden, Mega Man, UN Squadron, Contra, Golden Eye, Gauntlet, and the list went on and on. The deeper we got, the further we moved through the history of video games. It was like Disney World for gamers, going through some sort of hall of fame.

We must have tripped a wire or activated weight sensors because torches burst into flame like dominoes lighting our way. The bottom of the stairwell came up before we knew it. Lockers lined the walls of the dungeon like basement. Each one was equipped with a robotic suit, some kind of cybernetic exoskeleton meant for reinforcement. The top of the lockers had advanced Jackers that looked more like the days of Oculus Rift virtual reality visors, covering the entirety of your head. Their nicknames were Cycs after Cyclops, the X-men mutant.

Knightcr@wler was the only one not fascinated by the gear. On the far side of the room was a door with a submarine hatch wheel. It was brutishly intimidating. Knightcr@wler was attempting to open it. "It won't budge, give me some help." We all wandered over and tried to manhandle the steel. It wouldn't move an inch.

"We've got to use the suits," Knightcr@wler said. I walked back to one of the awaiting armors. It appeared as though I could sit down into it. I turned to face Kira who was visibly nervous. She watched me with bewildered eyes. I breathed in deep and sat down sinking into the metallic skeleton. My eyes stayed closed hoping that the machine wouldn't crush my body, yet nothing happened. I was sitting in powerless metal that wanted nothing to do with me.

"Guess she doesn't want you inside her... no surprise there," Phantom said smirking. He ran over to the one closest to him and tried to sit down, but was met with the same result. "I've seen this happen once before. From my extensive experience, I believe the robotics are most likely lesbian. Kira give her a try."

Kira gave a little smile and sat in one on the far side of the room closest to the door. Again the metal lay dead to the world. We all started laughing hysterically in the frames of lifeless machines. The only one that was silent and standing was Knightcr@wler. He was still observing the exoskeleton that he stood in front of. "It can't be," he said taking his Jackers off of his head. He folded in the arms of the glasses and placed them face forward in a cubby just above the Cycs. A bar on top of the locker energized and started to upload information as though it was reading them. The dimensions of the cybernetic exoskeleton began shifting on their own. Then a voice spoke, "Brett Henderson alias Knightcr@wler, enter player one when ready."

Knightcr@wler sat down inside the machine and it twirled around his legs and torso. A tentacle grabbed the Cycs and placed them on his head while a metallic spinal cord latched to his back, securing his helmet in place. His hands were covered in cybernetic gauntlets that he now squeezed, watching them in astonishment. It was the closest thing I had ever seen to a real life Robocop. He must have realized the same thing because he said, "Dead or Alive you're coming with me!" He jumped up, the force of his movements being magnified almost made him crash into the ceiling. It took him a second, but he was able to stabilize, getting used to his own power, "jump on in guys, the water is just right," he said.

Within an instant we all had our Jackers linked to the lockers and our machines activated welcoming us. My movements were still fluid but amplified. The Cycs were just like Jackers except the overlays were flawless. I had no ability to turn VEG off and I couldn't distinguish between virtual augmentation and reality. The one relieving aspect of the reality was that I could still see my friend's faces. The overlay showed their suits but not their helmets.

The suits took a little getting used to. It was Knightcr@wler who approached the door first turning the submarine style wheel with ease. Steam jets shot off from the metallic gap and the door hissed, swinging open to reveal a beautiful underground paradise.

It was recognizable to everyone the moment we stepped through. It was the realm of free play from Enders Game. In front of us, lay the giant's corpse, now covered in overgrowth. It was just like it was described in the book. "I don't get it," Phantom said looking out over the lush green hill that was once the living giant. "Why bring us here? It's that stupid free play crap that helps Ender not be so noob. What does this have to do with our quest?"

Knightcr@wler was silent; he sat observing the environment for a bit. "There's got to be something different... something that doesn't belong. It's a game, some kind of puzzle, but why? I figured that the staircase was the equivalent to Ender passing through the end of the world door... but for some reason it seems that we are back to square one," Knightcr@wler said confused.

We walked for a minute around the environment before Knightcr@wler noticed it, "Up there on the giant's chest," he said, pointing at two large cups resting side by side on top of the hill. A gold trimmed placard rested on the ground in front of the two drinks that read: "*CHOOSE.*" Both cups were identical in shape and size. One contained a bubbling green liquid and the other a bright purple substance with streaks of white lights swirling within. Phantom jumped up without hesitation and picked up the cup on the right, which was filled with the bubbling green liquid. He drank deep until the acids burned through his core spilling his dissolving intestines on the ground in front of us. His exoskeleton reacted forcing him to shake as if he were convulsing. It was pleasurable watching Phantom die and I think we all smiled a bit.

Upon his death he had to exit the area, he was allowed to come back but was banned from a second attempt. "Noob," Kira said smiling as he approached.

"What? You knew one of us had to do it," Phantom said to rebuttal.

"Alright look, let's analyze this. The giant gives every kid at battle school two drinks and whichever one you choose is death," Knightcr@wler said pacing around the cups. "The giant is dead though but yet the choice remains."

"I don't get that anyways, why did free play have the giant's drink game for every child?" Phantom asked. Knightcr@wler walked up to the purple drink and stared into the swirling lights lost in a trance. "The game was designed to manipulate the children. My guess is that the giant represents the children's superiors. Colonel Graff and so on, the puppeteers so to speak that are controlling the games. They are giving the children two choices that they think will prepare them for winning the war, yet AI is the one that creates free play with its own intentions," Knightcr@wler said walking over toward the giant's skull. He stopped at the eye. "Ender beat the giant by clawing through his eye to kill him. Choosing the path that the structured system couldn't predict. The giant may represent the Generals that took advantage of Ender but the giant was still created by artificial intelligence that understood maybe more than they did. An AI that understood more than Ender did about himself, the first ghost in the shell." Knightcr@wler walked back to stand in front of the cups. "If the two drinks represent choices made by the system, then they were destined to lead to Earth's destruction, and ultimately death. The elders think inside the box and try to mold the youth, to optimize their performance within the guidelines of their strategies, which were wrong. They don't factor in the idea of evolution and how quick it occurs. What was good for the youth in their day is never what is good for the youth of the future. You must adapt with change or it will overtake you…"

"Jesus Knightcr@wler, get to the point. If you know what to do, then do it," Phantom said annoyed.

"That's just it, the giant is dead. I don't know what to do. If we choose, we still choose an outdated strategy for the game and we die as you did," Knightcr@wler said.

"Well, regardless, one of us is going to have to try the other drink," Kira said, stepping up to the glowing purple cup. She picked it up with both hands. Knightcr@wler looked like he wanted to object but then decided not to intervene. She gulped down a good portion of the liquid and then dropped the cup back to its resting place. Her insides didn't melt which was a good sign. "I can't move," she said with a strange look on her face. Then her body began to expand. She started blowing up like a balloon, doubling in size until she exploded.

"Well great. Two down," I said. Kira reset and made it back up to the top of the hill in no time.

"Kira, that was the biggest I think I have ever seen your breasts," Phantom said smiling. Kira charged at him, knocking him down to the ground. "Relax, Jesus, it was just a joke." Phantom said fighting her off.

"I liked you better when you were dead," she said shooting him a nasty look.

"Shut up guys, let me think," Knightcr@wler said.

"Well there is only one thing left we can do," I said. "I'll try mixing them?" I said looking at Knightcr@wler.

"I thought about that, I don't know if it will work and if we lose you then we only have one more life left," Knightcr@wler said. "If we all die then who knows if we will ever be allowed back in."

"There has got to be some kind of reset. I'm sure we could try tomorrow. Charles wouldn't let you come this far to lock you out just because you didn't get his quest right the first time," Kira said.

"Alright then, here it goes," I said stepping up between the two drinks. I picked up the purple drink and poured it into the green drink and it began boiling with an eerie glow. The boiling subsided and I was left with brown thick goo.

"Bottoms up," I said taking down as much as I could stomach. I then proceeded to vomit out all of my insides until my character was as flat as paper, bones and all. We had one life left. I made my way back to the starting point and hustled back up the hill to meet the others. Kira and Phantom were lying on the ground taking a nap while Knightcr@wler was pondering over the drinks. "Maybe try and mix them the other way?" I said trying to help but Knightcr@wler brushed the comment aside.

Knightcr@wler sat in thought for a good thirty minutes dismissing any ideas that we gave him. Then he stood up, "I don't know if this will work but it's worth a try. At least it won't result in my death. Evo, give me a hand. Pick up the purple drink and come over here." Knightcr@wler picked up the green drink and headed over toward the mouth of the giant. I followed with the purple one. "On three pour it inside." He counted down and then we both poured the entirety of our drinks down the giant's throat.

The ground began to rumble, and tissue started to form on the giant's face. Teeth started to sprout and a tongue manifested. We all ran down the body to clear away from the reviving beast. He gagged, grasping for air, shaking in pain as the tissue darted down his body. Veins twirled around bone mass and muscles formed. Skin bubbled and took shape as he sat upright coughing out shrubs that once inhabited his carcass only moments ago. He clawed at his eye and screamed as he felt the void that Ender had caused before his death, reliving his final moments. Then he stopped, he sat motionless and regained his calm. His head hung low and he bellowed, "Who has revived me?"

Knightcr@wler stepped up and spoke, "I have."

The giant crawled toward us on all fours and looked directly at Knightcr@wler with his one good eye. "Why have you revived me?" he asked.

"Because, you weren't meant to die, you were built to enforce a failing system. You were a means to an end. Ender didn't mean to kill you; he meant to kill the system. He chose to survive," Knightcr@wler said.

The giant seemed satisfied and continued, "Answer these two questions and you may proceed. Answer incorrectly and you will perish." Knightcr@wler nodded. "In Ender's Game, who is the enemy?" the giant asked.

"That's easy, the Buggers." Phantom said.

Knightcr@wler gave Phantom a death stare. Then he looked back at the giant. He appeared calm and collective. "We are... I mean... human beings," Knightcr@wler said.

The giant nodded and asked another, "Who is Ender trying to save?"

Knightcr@wler didn't even take time to think, he spoke without question. "Humanity."

The giant smiled and then opened his mouth. We all shielded ourselves from the attack but it never came. A loud thunderous crash shook the ground. When we looked, the giant's mouth was contorted open. It was wide and gaping, his tongue extended outwards, revealing an entrance into his body. Knightcr@wler stepped forward and we all followed him into the depths of the giant.

There was a stink to the bowels of the giant that hung upon my nostrils. It encouraged the gag reflexes. The body was void of organs, eerie and hollow with just the foul breeze of breath whisking by. The lining of the rib cage was visible. It pulsed to life with the rhythmic inhale and exhale of giant.

Resting near where I imagined the pelvis might have been was a cloaked figure in all black holding a sword with both hands. Its head was tilted down slightly, allowing the hood to cover its face. Its blade's tip rested firmly on the ground. Behind the cloaked figure was a chest. I could see the excitement in everyone's eyes. We all knew it was there but tried to act cool about it. The end was within our grasps.

When we stepped closer, the mysterious figure spoke, "only one may approach." The voice startled, and struck a chord of fear inside. I wasn't going to be the first to volunteer but I also didn't want to appear a coward in front of Kira. While the debate ensued, Knightcr@wler stepped up and saved me from my dilemma.

He ran at the figure and as he approached the exoskeleton suit armed. Armor shot out locking in place over his entire body so that he was covered from head to toe in steel. It scaled his body like a dragon. Knightcr@wler jumped at the figure, his fists both extended outwards as he dove into a twirling attack. The enemy slipped right at an incredible speed, slashing downwards with his sword into the center of Knightcr@wler's chest. The blow sent him bouncing off the ground head first into the treasure chest. He screamed out in pain, real pain. The figure grabbed him by the leg and tossed his body back to us. "Brett!" Phantom screamed. Phantom grabbed him by the arms and shook him.

"I'm alright," he coughed a bit. "The suit took a lot of the blow but damn this is no joke. What kind of game is this?" When we looked up the figure was in its resting position again with his hands gripping the butt end of the sword and the tip resting once again on the ground in front of him. "I saw his face, he said in a whisper. It was someone I knew," he managed to say between coughs. "Someone I hated... how could it... how could it know...?"

"He's mine," Phantom said, taking a different approach. He broke one of the bones from the giant's rib cage and wielded it like a weapon. Phantom was cautious. He approached slow, tiptoeing forward till he saw a reaction. When he got close, close enough to taste battle, he became enraged and struck wildly. The bone shattered to pieces when it collided with the sharpened steel sword. Phantom threw the remaining fragment in his hand at the figures face. It was meant to distract as he slid at its ankles. The dark one danced around him with ease, smacking his chest with the butt end of its sword. Then it swiped its sword low along the ground taking Phantom's legs out from under him. He was on the floor in an instant. Before he could regain his footing the figure tossed him like a rag doll, sending him back out to join Knightcr@wler.

Phantom was in a daze when we approached. His eyes were locked upon a distant memory. He was broken, not physically but mentally. "My father... right over there was my father. Five feet from me and in the flesh.... Five feet from me and I couldn't touch him... couldn't cut him... couldn't slit his throat, couldn't..." he trailed off into a loop of psychotic fantasy.

We only knew bits and pieces of Phantom's past but we did know that his father wasn't the best of men. He was abusive to both he and his mother. He left before Phantom was ever able to repay the pain he had caused him. How could this thing know? I looked up at Kira. She returned my gaze and knew right away saying, "Don't."

I looked at the figure who was a statue once again. I didn't turn back to Kira, "I have to," I said, and walked toward the dark one.

Courage escaped my limbs, but curiosity drove me forward. The cloaked figure's hood trapped shadows in its depths. They swirled around its face like dark dreams as its head rose to my approach. Chaos ensued, dark blots bounced and collided at random, but near the eyes and spreading fast like cancer was order. It was subtle at first; almost unrecognizable but facial features began manifesting. The body doubled in size. I knew before the transformation completed. I was pitted against myself ages ago. The loser: the worthless, good for nothing gamer. *"All you do is sit around all day on that damn computer,"* my father's words echoed in my head. Too scared to fight my own battles, too fat to take control of my life, too disgusting to make friends.

I swung my fist without thought, a concoction of hatred and force boiled in my knuckles. The absence of contact ignited an even deeper rage within. Something struck me from the back and sent me head first into a wall. The pain was distant, and the rage consumed on, devouring the entirety of my being. I struck the wall with my fists, slamming them against it repeatedly until the pain and rage brewed into one.

As a child, all I wanted was to gain acceptance, but I was *"too fat and too stupid."* I was too fat and too stupid to please anyone. Gaming became my escape, the first place I made friends. Reality slipped away as I indulged in fantasy. Relationships crumbled as I climbed in virtual rank. I was too fat and too stupid to see it. I felt the shame. The same shame my parents must have felt toward me.

"I can't get up," the figure said taunting me in that whimpering weak voice that I knew all too well. Rage clouded my vision, invading my mind. The voice was close enough to taste the metallic breath. A backwards lunge was expected. I pushed with all of my might toward the wall, finding footing to leap off of. The figure's sword missed by inches, as I flipped backwards over its head. There was my chance. I let the fury build from my core. Turning all the shame, doubt, and pain into a weapon as I struck. My fist collided with nothing, missing my mirrored self by close to a foot. My ancient twin was faster than any enemy I had ever faced. It attacked me from the rear. This time the blow came to my head, it rattled my thoughts and flooded my senses. "EVO!" someone screamed. Someone distant.

I knew that voice though, that sweet voice, that caring voice, that voice that loved me as I had never loved myself. *Kira...* her fear for me coated my name's sound. That one word bullied its way into my core, extinguishing my fire, cooling me to an eerie calm. Thought turned inside my mind once more, and focus filled my senses.

I was deep in strategy, rummaging through everything that had happened. *It is just a game. There is a way to win. This is the free play game. Ender chooses love. Ender chooses love*, I repeated to myself as I turned back toward the figure. It looked up, peering into my soul. His hands rested firmly on his blade in his original position. They began to raise as I stepped forward. I wasn't focused on the blade, I was focused on the boy... The boy I hated. The boy that I could never forgive for what he had done with his life. The boy I had been ashamed of. That was it though; I was just a boy. A boy that didn't relate. There was nothing wrong with me. This wasn't about defeat. It was about acceptance.

"I love you..." I whispered, barely able to stomach the words. I couldn't look into my own eyes and say it. That is all I wanted to hear. All those years it was all I craved. For some reason it was all I wanted to say. I looked up into my own eyes. A scared lost boy stared back. He wasn't pathetic, he wasn't too fat or too stupid, he was just a boy. A boy looking to belong. "I love you," I said hugging the cloaked figure. It sat motionless for a second and then turned. Its arms were still raised to strike but facing away from me. They came down with an incredible speed, crashing into the top of the treasure chest. It shattered into a million pieces. Then the figure turned back toward me and froze back into his ominous pose.

The chest had an eerie blue glow resonating from within. The fables were true; a blue tinted sword lay within. Silver thread rose from hilt to cross-guard in an intricate fashion. The blade was almost sapphire in nature but strong like steel. It had the entire universe spanning its length. I grabbed it with both hands and felt the power of it pulsing within. Whether it was my imagination or not I knew that this blade was unique, for it was not just a blade. It represented the friendship and the love that had flourished from our gangs first meeting. It was an item that united us. We had completed something that no one else could and in doing so I had completed myself.

About the Author

My intentions were to dazzle, to amaze, even to entice the reader with tales of grandeur in my bio. But it's a cup of coffee past sunrise and I need sleep. The idea of defining myself on a page sickens me. It curdles in my creative cortex. I'm not a writer. I'm a storyteller. I enjoy losing myself in that place where you're walking with the story. It's leading, an infinite wonder lies just beyond. You can't see it yet but you trust that it's there. Maybe it's the illusive ADD that I was diagnosed with as a child that allowed for me to lose myself in stories. I just thought it was called being creative in the good old days. One constant is clear to me; I want to read my story as much as you do. Somewhere, hidden in those pages you will find pieces of me. Read on, I know I will.

That is who I am, a man attempting to enjoy the endless exploration of his mind. Facebook or Google searches will answer any other questions you have about me. Maybe even an old profile on match.com, but don't tell my wife if you discover it. Or, we could leave a little mystery, a little whisper of magic to entice fantasy and make believe into filling that ancient void. We are all curious children somewhere; my stories are attempts at awakening yours.